O, Gayest Love of Bethlehem

A Long-Lost Tale of
Gay Christian Romance
during the First Christmas

Second Edition, The New King Jamie Version

Reverend Richard B. Hard

This book is primarily intended for readers over the age of 18 and with a sense of humor. If you are not yet 18 years old, consider consulting your parents and/or legal guardians for advice on how to proceed. If you lack a sense of humor, stop reading immediately and seek help from a therapist.

ISBN 979-8-9938550-0-4 (e-book)
ISBN 979-8-9938550-1-1 (paperback)
ISBN 979-8-9938550-2-8 (hardback)

Introduction

As Christmas approached at the gift workshop in the North Pole, Mrs. Claus became so consumed with her bookkeeping and baking that she began neglecting the needs of her partner. Consequently, Daddy Santa began to feel lonely and developed an irrepressible urge: the urge to take advantage of their open relationship and devote himself to his favorite elf, Tybel.

During Tybel's government-mandated thirty-minute lunch break, Daddy Santa pulled him aside and requested that he take the rest of the day off for an extensive, in-person performance review. After engaging in this especially deep review of Tybel's performance, he and Daddy Santa lay naked in the California king bed in the luxury suite above the workshop. Splayed across the red satin sheets, they reveled in their post-coital stupor. A gentle snow fell outside, but in bed together, Daddy Santa and Tybel kept each other warm.

Tybel went to the bathroom to wash up, and when he returned, he climbed back into bed, curled up next to Daddy Santa, and ran his fingers through his partner's fluffy, white beard.

"It truly is a shame," Tybel said, "that we cannot tell the world the truth about our sexuality."

Daddy Santa scoffed. "Why would we want to be honest with the people of the world? Not that long ago, some cable TV pundits freaked out over the mere suggestion that I might be Black! Could you imagine the reaction if people learned that I'm a polyamorous, bisexual Daddy?"

"I suppose you are right," Tybel said with a sigh.

"And don't even get me started on the extremely online kids these days! Why, Tybel, they would take one look at our love, divorce it from all its context, label it sexual misconduct, and then demand that I resign from all my responsibilities as Santa Claus!"

Tybel rolled his eyes. "Okay Boomer."

Daddy Santa laughed, and stroked Tybel's soft, supple body. He was a tall and sexy elf of the Tolkien variety, with long, hairless legs; tan, smooth skin; and luscious, blond curly hair. Daddy Santa kissed his neck and licked his Adam's apple.

"Stop, Daddy Santa!" Tybel groaned, pushing him away. "I didn't put hickeys on my Christmas wish list!"

Daddy Santa sat up, annoyed. "Well, what do you want for Christmas, then? I already gave you the biggest package of them all…"

Tybel rolled his eyes again. "I already said what I want, but I guess you weren't listening. I want the world to know about our relationship. I want them to know that I love you, that you love me, and to understand that there is nothing wrong with the love we feel for each other. Why can't we show our true selves to the world?"

Daddy Santa wrapped his thick, brawny arms around Tybel and pulled him close.

"Oh, Tybel, you are so young, innocent, and naïve. Our love is just one of many that the world will never know. It is sad, but it is the truth: too many people remain intolerant of gay love for us to associate it with anything related to religious holidays. The erasure of homosexuality is a story as old as Christmas itself! After all, that's why the Council of Nicaea removed all the gay stuff from the story of the birth of Baby Jesus."

A puzzled expression flashed across Tybel's face. "What gay stuff?"

Daddy Santa gasped. "You don't know? The other gay elves never told you the full, *true* story of Christmas?"

"No…What are you saying?" Tybel asked. "Do you mean that Jesus was gay?"

Daddy Santa guffawed boisterously: "Ho, ho, ho! Don't be ridiculous! Jesus wasn't gay. He was just a young man who wore long robes and exclusively hung out with other young men as they marauded about all the trendy neighborhoods in Judea to spread their message of love."

"That sounds pretty gay to me."

Daddy Santa shook his head. "Well, he wasn't. Jesus was as straight as Shawn Mendes. But the original story of Jesus's birth had a gay subplot that was omitted from the Bible to preserve heteronormativity, maintain traditional family values, and prevent a complete and total collapse of Western Civilization."

"Really?" Tybel exclaimed, his blue eyes widening with delight.

"Why, yes! The story is only known today because gay men have passed it down from generation to generation through our oral traditions."

Tybel scrunched his face in confusion. "But then how come I don't already know this story? You know that I practice *all* our oral traditions!"

Daddy Santa chuckled. "Not *those* oral traditions, Tybel! I mean storytelling. The gay subplot of the first Christmas was never written down. Instead, it's been memorized and recited by older gay men to younger gay men over the course of many centuries."

Tybel gazed up at his lover, his buff muscles, his jolly cheekbones, his masculine jaw. Ever since Daddy Santa began his semaglutide injections, his iconic potbelly had shrunk, leaving him with an especially charming dad bod. The other gay elves would eye Daddy Santa all day, dreaming about what lay beneath his red suit. Tybel was one of the lucky few to know Daddy Santa in the flesh, and he never missed an opportunity to indulge in his most lustful desires.

"Please, Daddy Santa," Tybel begged. "Can you tell me the true story of Christmas tonight? I promise to be a good boy and stay in bed with you all night long!"

Daddy Santa stared at Tybel longingly. He leaned over and gave Tybel a kiss on the lips. Then he positioned himself above the elf and lowered his hands down to Tybel's round, firm ass.

"Oh Tybel," Daddy Santa said. "I'll tell you everything you want to know about the gay love that was shared during the first Christmas."

He kissed Tybel on the forehead.

"But first," Daddy Santa added, "I want to show you how glorious that love must have felt..."

An hour later, after much moaning and pleasure, their limbs still entangled with one another, Daddy Santa began to tell Tybel the following story.

The Innkeeper

Much of the story of the first Christmas is widely known: the immaculate conception, the birth of Jesus in a manger, the escape from King Herod, and so forth.

However, in the Bible and in other accounts of Jesus's birth, details about the modest inn and its generous innkeeper are scant.

That is for a reason, as the inn was not a typical business establishment. In fact, unbeknownst to most authorities, this inn was a secret refuge for the LGBTQ+ community in Judea and beyond.

Every year, gay boys and girls who had been disowned by their family would come to the inn, looking for a safe place to stay. The establishment took in these homeless youths and gave them shelter, clean clothes, and a path forward in life.

Only gay Judeans and their allies knew the truth about this inn. To outsiders, it was one of many lodging houses for transitory people in Bethlehem. But to those in the know, the safe haven had a beautiful name: The Butterfly Sanctuary.

The Butterfly Sanctuary was a two-story structure made of mudbrick and stone. It had sixteen rooms, each furnished with a cot, a comforter, and a candelabra. The rooms looked out on a courtyard with a pond, a well, and a small fountain, letting guests relax and hear the calming trickle of running water. In its time, The Butterfly Sanctuary was one of the most highly respected and talked about LGBTQ+ destinations east of Byzantium.

The inn was also situated in one of the trendier areas of Bethlehem, although back in those days, most people didn't fully grasp the concept of "trendy." One might even suggest the neighborhood was gentrifying, in part thanks to an influx of gay Judeans who wanted roads made of stone instead of dirt, murals and frescos in common areas, and teahouses with quality tea from the East.

Here, in this small corner of the Roman Empire, LGBTQ+ culture thrived, even though its existence always remained discrete. And while two women founded the inn and initiated its mission, because of the patriarchal laws of the age, one man served as the official innkeeper and owner in all business records. His name was Abrahamus, and he would become a legend in his time, known throughout all the underground gay networks of the Roman Empire.

But at the time of Jesus's birth, Abrahamus was struggling with a predicament: despite being rescued himself by the founders of The Butterfly Sanctuary and becoming its finest employee, Abrahamus remained deep in the closet.

Two weeks before the events of the first Christmas, while Abrahamus was fast asleep, the most beautiful angel appeared in his room amidst a ball of glowing white light. The angel had long, flowing white hair and donned a luxurious white gown under a black vest bedazzled with glittering gemstones.

"Greetings, Abrahamus," the angel said. "I bring thee good news."

Abrahamus stirred from his sleep and looked up at the angel.

"Who goes there?" he asked.

"It is I, Ezekliana, an angel of the Lord," the heavenly figure said. "My preferred pronouns are they/them/their, for the Lord created me as intersex and non-binary, and he commanded me to live my life as my true self, as he does command all human beings."

Abrahamus understood and recognized Ezekliana's preferred pronouns, for he respected the will of the Lord, and also because he wasn't a jerk.

"Why are you here?" Abrahamus asked.

"I have come to you with a message from the Lord," Ezekliana said, and they whipped their hair back so that it shimmered in the bright light. "In a fortnight, two weary travelers shall come to you from Nazareth. You must help them find shelter by whatever means necessary. It is of the utmost concern for the Lord, and if possible, He asks that you make a reservation on their behalf."

Abrahamus bowed his head. "I will do so, for I have great respect for the Lord."

Ezekliana continued: "To ensure safe refuge for these travelers, the Lord will submit to you a reservation through Travelocity."

Abrahamus cocked his head to the side. "Travelocity? What is that?"

Ezekliana smacked their forehead. "Oh, silly me! Travelocity is not around for another two millennia. I'm so sorry. You must understand: in Heaven, the space-time continuum is nonlinear, so we sometimes mix up the availability of inventions at a particular moment on Earth."

Abrahamus stared at Ezekliana with a look of pure confusion.

"Never mind all that," they continued. "How do you normally reserve a room in advance for expected travelers?"

"I write a note to remind myself," Abrahamus replied.

Ezekliana nodded. "Very good. In that case, Abrahamus, the Lord asks you to write a note to reserve a room for these weary travelers. They will come to you in the evening, and the woman shall be with child. Save for them your finest room, and make sure they stay safe."

Abrahamus yawned, for he suddenly felt very tired. "Yes, yes, you can assure the Lord that I shall do so. Two travelers in a fortnight, one a woman with a child."

With a sly smile, Ezekliana replied: "The Lord thanks you for your generosity, and He shall reward you with many joyful pleasures…"

And just as suddenly as they appeared, they vanished.

Abrahamus plunged back into bed. He was exhausted. Earlier in the day, he had cleaned all the rooms as well as the stables in the back, and he'd have another busy day tomorrow. Soon, he drifted back to sleep.

In the morning, when Abrahamus awoke, he felt groggy and sore. He was not a young man anymore—after all, last year, he had reached the age of 30. His hair still lacked any shades of gray, and because of his constant cleaning of the inn and the stables, he had a noticeably fit body: bulging biceps, vascular forearms, chiseled abdominals.

In modern parlance, he was a hunk.

He went downstairs and wrote himself a note on a piece of papyrus:

Reserve room for travelers in a fortnight.

He placed the note on a table by the entrance to the inn. Then he proceeded to the courtyard, where numerous guests already sat about, many of them gay men drinking tea and gossiping with one another. But Abrahamus did not interact with any of these men; instead, he picked up his broom and began to sweep, continuing his never-ending effort to keep the courtyard clean.

Some of the male guests eyed Abrahamus, but Abrahamus disregarded the attention. He was too scared to interact with these strangers, largely due to his troubled past...

Abrahamus had grown up on a date farm in a village not far from Bethlehem. He was the youngest of seventeen siblings. As a shy child with a bashful demeanor and a lisp, his brothers and sisters looked down on him and teased him frequently.

Every year during the harvest, a group of his siblings would take advantage of Abrahamus's naïveté. After filling hundreds of baskets with dates, they'd claim their father had asked him to sort and pit every last one. For days on end and all alone, Abrahamus would sift through the dates, while his siblings ran off and played.

8

As time passed, his sisters were married off and his brothers pursued work in larger cities, but Abrahamus remained. He tended to the dates and cared for his parents. Even though he understood that his siblings had played a trick on him, he had come to enjoy handling the dates by himself, and so he continued the work without complaints.

Abrahamus rarely left the farm and only occasionally interacted with the other young men and women in his village. All the men were boorish and only ever talked of women, a topic he found disinteresting. Some of the women treated him kindly, but his highly devout parents discouraged him from fraternizing with them unless he had a desire to marry. For some reason, unlike most men his age, he did not possess an eagerness to pursue women romantically.

So Abrahamus lived a quiet life of solitude, fully focused on his dates, his chores, the animals on the farm, and tending to his parents as they aged. He felt happy enough, but at times, he worried that his life would forever feel so limited, so confined to this small corner of the world…

One day, a mysterious traveler on a horse stopped by the entrance to the farm. Abrahamus was sitting in the front yard, surrounded by baskets of dates, when he appeared. Dressed in an alluring pink garb and riding a black stallion, the man appeared to be an Arab, perhaps some kind of royalty— Abrahamus was not sure, for he had only heard of Arabs.

Abrahamus was immediately intrigued. The young man seemed to be about the same age as him. He had dark hair, piercing green eyes, and a neatly trimmed black beard. The man walked with so much confidence, you could believe he was seven feet tall, even though he actually was quite a bit shorter than Abrahamus.

This mysterious traveler approached the shady grove of palm trees where Abrahamus sat.

"Excuse me, sir," the traveler asked with a flirtatious lilt. "Can you tell me the way to Jerusalem?"

Abrahamus was stunned and unable to speak. He was too entranced by the traveler, so he merely pointed in the correct direction.

The mysterious man grinned and gave Abrahamus a small bow. And just as quickly as he had appeared, the man returned to his horse and left.

All day, the vision of this mysterious traveler lurked in Abrahamus's mind. The memory instilled in him feelings he had never felt before, emotions that words could not describe. Throughout the rest of the day, whenever Abrahamus thought of the man—the accent, the plump lips, the beautiful smile—his muscles tightened. A warm feeling would grow in his chest, and soon, he'd also feel the hardening of the appendage in the nether regions of his body—an appendage that his devout family had taught him hardly anything about besides urination. Sheltered and confused, he kept his thoughts and feelings to himself.

That night, as he lay in bed, thoughts of the man came to Abrahamus, and his appendage grew hard again. He felt deeply ashamed. If someone entered the room, he worried they might notice. After all, his appendage had grown shockingly large, creating a mountain under his blanket.

He knew he had to tame his appendage. He started with gentle strokes, an act that felt surprisingly enjoyable. He began to rub his appendage faster and faster, gripping the long, girthy shaft tightly before gently touching its tip, which he found gave him the most pleasure.

The harder he rubbed, the more the mysterious traveler captivated him. He closed his eyes and pictured the two of them, standing next to each other, with Abrahamus running his hands along the man's gorgeous face, touching his lips and feeling their voluptuous shape. The man opened his mouth, stuck out his tongue, and seductively licked the phalanxes of Abrahamus's fingers. And then he imagined his hands moving along the man's limber body, around his shoulders, behind his back, down to his plump bottom, which he grabbed with delight.

Abrahamus groaned with pleasure, his hands working faster and faster, until suddenly, he felt something strange and sticky.

He opened his eyes and looked down at his hand. A white substance had ejaculated out of his appendage, contaminating his fingers, his groin, and his blanket. The substance smelled funny. He did not like it, and he felt even more deeply ashamed.

He used his blanket to rub the substance off his hands and groin, but the stickiness remained in his thick, coiled pubic hair. He didn't know what to do. As he lay in bed debating how to clean himself, he became more and more tired, exhausted from taming his appendage. He knew he'd have to bathe and cleanse himself in the morning, so he placed the soiled blanket beside his bed and fell asleep.

The next morning, the soiled blanket was gone. He put on his robe and went to fetch some water to bathe, but in the backyard, he saw his mother and father talking furtively and intensely. His mother held the soiled blanket and was showing it to his father.

When they saw him, his father scowled.

"Son, what did you do last night? What did you do to your blanket?"

Until then, Abrahamus had a very trusting relationship with his parents, having never lied to them.

He knew that his parents would not approve of his nighttime activities.

He knew that if he confessed his feelings for the mysterious traveler, he could permanently end his quiet life on the farm.

But Abrahamus was too innocent and too honest for his own good. With a look of shame, he told his father the truth: that he had envisioned a man in his sleep last night, and it caused his appendage to explode with white stickiness.

His father turned red with anger. "What do you mean, you saw a man?" he cried. "You know that is a sin! For this, you dishonor our family."

His mother wept, and Abrahamus began to cry, too. His father paced back and forth, exasperated.

"You must leave at once," he told Abrahamus. "You must go someplace else. We cannot have this type of sin in our home."

Abrahamus continued to cry, and he felt great shame, but he also believed his father was right. He knew his feelings were a sin in the eyes of his parents and forbidden by the laws of the land. He was thankful they did not tell anyone, and so he packed his things and left quietly that same morning, heading to the nearby town of Bethlehem.

In Bethlehem, he found The Butterfly Sanctuary. He was wandering the streets on his second night, still without shelter, when two women approached him and asked if he needed a place to stay. Their names were Dinah and Lara, the widows who founded the inn.

Dinah had inherited the property from her husband and continued to act its unofficial proprietress. She was a tall woman with short, dark hair who was often curt and direct, but to Abrahamus, she was always kind. Lara was blond, fair skinned, and shorter, and she walked gracefully everywhere she went. Her backstory was unknown to most in Bethlehem, for she had unexpectedly arrived at the inn not long after the passing of Dinah's husband. Abrahamus would later learn that Lara and Dinah had grown up together in Jericho, once being close childhood friends. And after the two reunited in Bethlehem, they had become inseparable.

At the time, the inn was mostly empty, so Abrahamus took a room all to himself. For the next few days, Abrahamus moped about the building, rarely daring to go outside. Out of pity, Dinah offered him a job that would include his room and board, knowing that she and Lara would benefit from having a man as the face of the business. He gladly accepted this offer and soon became a fixture of their establishment.

Only over time would he discover the secret mission of The Butterfly Sanctuary. He eventually noticed that Dinah and Lara slept together every night, and that they often sought out and offered lodging to similar types of men and women: young, lost, and marginalized youth who were stranded without friends or family.

But even though he had much in common with his employer and their guests, he never confirmed his sexuality to anyone. He remained a quiet, masculine presence who greeted the many eclectic lodgers at the inn.

Still, every night, trouble returned to Abrahamus. Repeatedly, he dreamt of the mysterious traveler who had come on horseback: his gentle face, his long eyelashes, his delectable and grabbable buttocks. He would wake up in the morning, his appendage still hard, his mind still full of shame, until the feelings dissipated and he could focus on his tasks for the day—preparing rooms, sweeping the courtyard, and greeting guests as they arrived.

His humdrum life continued in this manner for seven years, with Abrahamus keeping his secret, never confirming what Lara, Dinah, and many guests already sensed: if another man ever shared his bed, he might possess the most animalistic instincts…

The Wise Men

For centuries, Biblical scholars have speculated about the identities of the three wise men in the story of Jesus's birth. Various names have been suggested over the years, including numerous historical figures. Perhaps these suggestions were innocent mistakes. But then again, perhaps historians put forth these names to cover up the true history of the wise men, and in particular, the identity of one of the most wild, magnificent LGBTQ+ icons of the ancient world: Prince Hamid Abgarid, second son of King Abgar Abgarid of the Mesopotamian Kingdom of Osroene.

Historians know little about Hamid, for even in his earliest days, he was a wanderlust vagabond, roaming the Middle East sporadically and leaving little trace of his adventures. As a child, he had grown fond of horses. By his teenage years, he was one of the best riders in the city of Edessa, the seat of the kingdom, located about 500 miles north of Judea. He had a staff of five men who managed his stables and all its livestock. Whenever he became bored of life in the capital, Hamid would mount one of his horses and set off on an adventure. Sometimes, he would bring along a male friend, too, testing them to see if he could keep up! But his male friends never could meet his high standards, for Hamid was the fastest rider in the land, and he liked to show off.

Hamid was a fan of the finer things in life. He had grown accustomed to silk from the East dyed the most startling colors: lime green, bright yellow, and his favorite color of all, pink.

As a prince, he was offered the finest tutors in the land, and he excelled academically. And despite his diminutive nature, he was a fierce warrior. Swift with a sword and agile in his legwork, he often caught opponents by surprise, although he never saw combat and only fought performatively with trainers who might have wanted him to win.

He was a cosmopolitan man for his time, and incredibly social, too. In his court, he had male friends and concubines, with whom he often spent the days. Together, they roamed the streets of Edessa as Hamid oversaw his affairs.

Although eccentric and often the subject of rumors, Prince Hamid was respected by the people of Edessa as someone who listened to others. Whether a miscreant youth in need of guidance or a crack in the aqueduct in need of repair, Hamid paid attention to problems and urged his father to address them. As the second son, he had no ambition to be King, but he still saw himself as a leader. For him, his duty was to serve all the subjects of the kingdom, no matter their status or standing.

Prince Hamid loved the world and all it had to offer, but as he grew older, he felt a desire for something more meaningful. He began to wonder how his life might look in five or ten years. Would he still have a flurry of male concubines, all eager to cater to his erotic desires? Would he still find joy in the luxuries of life? A sense of ennui grew within him, for he believed life was meant for more than just pleasure: that we all served a higher purpose, even if the exact nature of that purpose remained a mystery.

On the night that an angel of the Lord visited Prince Hamid, his mind was far from any thoughts of spiritual callings. Instead, he was entertaining two of his most cherished friends, the sons of noblemen from nearby cities: Imran and Balbazaar. Every few months, the three men would gather for an evening to explore the many delights of their anatomies.

All three were strapping young men, but they had their differences. Prince Hamid had soft, tan skin from his many baths and his use of the finest creams, while Imran and Balbazaar maintained gruffer, more masculine appearances. Imran was tall and lanky, often quiet, and kept a thick beard, while Balbazaar had a bulkier body, with thick arms, thick thighs, and a large, muscular chest.

In truth, Imran and Balbazaar both shared feelings for Prince Hamid, and he gave them both much joy. Although their traditional families encouraged them to take wives, these gentlemen enjoyed indulging in the most shocking acts with close male friends—especially Prince Hamid.

Prince Hamid, too, enjoyed toying with men like Imran and Balbazaar. He sensed their secret, suppressed desires and loved to awaken them. He liked to flirt, and once these men were sufficiently seduced, he would invite them to his room. He would let the men dominate his body, but he exerted his own influences over them: working their desires with his mouth or his bulbous butt cheeks. Despite the appearance of submission, he always retained control.

In modern parlance, he was a power bottom.

That evening, Prince Hamid had welcomed his friends into his bedroom. He laid down on his bed and spread his legs. He rested his feet on two ottomans that were spaced apart perfectly for opening himself up. Imran stood between the prince's legs and gently massage his neck, his back, and his sumptuous tush. Balbazaar, preferring to watch, leaned against a wall and placed his hand on his crotch.

Prince Hamid looked over at Balbazaar, his huge arms, his broad shoulders. Everything about Balbazaar was big, including his most private possession.

"Balbazaar, come here," Prince Hamid commanded.

Balbazaar smirked. He knew what was about to happen. Slowly, he walked toward Prince Hamid. As he did so, he loosened his undergarments and let them fall to the floor. His private instrument stood unveiled, gloriously erect and at least eight inches long. He positioned this device just above Prince Hamid's head.

"Is this what you were looking for?" Balbazaar asked.

Imran, still massaging Hamid, grinned. He, too, was becoming excited. He began to rub the prince more deeply, more aggressively. He climbed up onto the bed, straddled Hamid's posterior, and reached for the prince's shoulders.

Hamid lay very still, gazing up at Balbazaar.

"Come closer to my face," he demanded. "I want to give you a kiss."

Balbazaar rested his knee on the mattress, allowing the object of desire to graze Hamid's lips. Tilting his head back, Hamid touched it with the tip of his tongue, licking the foreskin.

At that moment, Imran pushed himself backwards and rubbed his groin against Hamid's tush. He pushed Hamid forward, so that the prince could more easily place his mouth around Balbazaar's object. Then Imran removed his pants and pressed his own large and hard instrument against the crevice in Hamid's bottom.

Everything then happened very fast: Balbazaar grabbed the back of Hamid's head, while Imran used his spit to lubricate his instrument. Hamid moaned with pleasure as his friends inserted themselves—and he made sure the pleasure was mutual. As the men gripped Hamid's head and hips and thrusted continuously, Hamid tightened his lips and clenched his butt, increasing the intensity of their acts.

The three men moved in one motion, forward and back, all of them wild with wanton felicity. Imran then reached beneath Hamid and tightened his fist around the prince's tool, enhancing his bliss even further. Pushing and pulling, they found their softest spots, the most pleasurable places to apply pressure, stroking and squeezing until they climaxed in unison. They collapsed on Hamid's soft sheets and exhaled in relief, overcome by an overwhelming sense of gratification.

As they recovered in this wonderous refractory period, a ball of light appeared by the window. Ezekliana found the young men lying together, naked. Imran and Hamid cuddled each other, while Balbazaar sat next to them, still touching himself. Oblivious to their heavenly visitor, Imran had smeared some of the semen from Hamid's orgasm onto his chest, and Hamid had started to lick the delectable confection out of Imran's fuzzy chest hair.

"Oh dear!" Ezekliana exclaimed. "Have I arrived at a bad time?"

The three men sat up with a start.

"What is this apparition?" Prince Hamid cried out. "Are you a demon?"

Ezekliana laughed. "Don't be silly, Prince Hamid! It is I, Ezekliana, an angel of the Lord."

Hamid leaned forward, while Imran and Balbazaar stared in astonishment. None of them had seen an angel before, but only Hamid had the courage to face one.

"What do you seek, messenger of the Lord?" Hamid asked. "Speak! I command thee!"

Sensing the powerful, unvarnished nature of the prince, Ezekliana became flustered.

"Well, a child of the Lord is to be born of a virgin in three days' time. He shall be born in Judea, in the city of Bethlehem. The Lord asks you to witness this birth and welcome him into this world with gifts, for he is the son of God—the Messiah—and he shall lead the world on a path toward truth and righteousness."

"I know the town of Bethlehem," Prince Hamid replied. "It is a town with many people. How will I find this child?"

Ezekliana gestured up to the evening sky.

"You must follow the star in the sky, the one that shines more brightly than the others. The star shall lead you to this child. And there, you shall find other sources of joy, too…"

Ezekliana raised their eyebrows in a suggestive manner. Prince Hamid laughed.

"Other sources of joy? What does that mean?"

But Ezekliana did not answer. Instead, they simply grinned and faded into the orb of light, vanishing as quickly as they had appeared.

With a sense of embarrassment, Imran grabbed the bedsheet to wipe the remaining semen from his chest. Balbazaar sat motionless, shocked. He had finally stopped fondling himself.

"Was that truly an angel of the Lord?" he asked.

Hamid turned to face Balbazaar. "Of course! Do we have any reason to doubt?"

Balbazaar blushed. "No…I have no doubt…but, to be honest, I did not believe angels were real."

Hamid sighed. As much as he appreciated his friends, he sometimes resented their inadequacy. They had all been educated by some of the finest scholars and tutors, but Imran and Balbazaar had never branched out and explored the world. Their understanding of spirituality came primarily from conversations at dinner parties or the lectures of priests. Neither of them had thought much about anything beyond the borders of the kingdom, let alone celestial beings.

"I must obey the angel," Hamid said. "But I do not wish to travel alone. Having been to Bethlehem, I know the way, and it is a long but safe journey. But I shall feel the tediousness of the distance if I travel by myself."

Balbazaar and Imran sat in silence.

"I should want two friends to accompany me," Hamid continued, trying to egg an answer out of them.

Imran gulped.

"Hamid, I should love to accompany you, but—"

"But what?"

Imran hesitated. Balbazaar fidgeted.

"I think Imran fears you might abandon us," Balbazaar added. "You always travel so fast on horseback and become so impatient with others. And any time you meet a man you fancy, you abandon your friends and run astray. We wouldn't want to be left alone and lost in the desert."

O, Gayest Love of Bethlehem

Prince Hamid took Balbazaar's hand. He sat up and gazed into his deep, dark brown eyes, then leaned forward and kissed him on the lips. Hamid then pivoted toward Imran and admired his strong cheekbones and his black, curly hair. He placed his arm around Imran, caressing him, and leaned over to kiss him, too.

"I know that I am often afflicted with the sin of impatience," he said. "And I am not one to overlook an opportunity to chase my pursuits. But I will never leave the two of you unless I have your permission. We are bonded as our closest friends—no, something more than just friends! I would never want to hurt either of you."

Imran snuggled up close to Hamid's chest. Balbazaar laid down alongside Hamid, too, and wrapped his arms around him.

"We shall leave tomorrow morning," Hamid said. "It has been many months since I have had an adventure. I am eager to see this child of the Lord and the mysterious 'joy' that the angel promised, whatever that might be."

The three of them cuddled one another as they drifted off to sleep, the moonlight streaming down through the bedroom window. In the sky above, a guiding star shone brightly, ready to lead these sexy wise men to the many delightful surprises awaiting them in Bethlehem...

The Travelers

Due to some additional carousing in the middle of the night, Imran, Balbazaar, and Prince Hamid slept in the next morning. By the time they awoke, the sun had already risen well above the horizon. Recalling the message of the angel, the three men prepared for their journey to Bethlehem.

"If this is the child of the Lord, should we not bring him quality gifts?" Balbazaar asked.

For once, Prince Hamid felt that Balbazaar had made a good point. He leaned over and opened a set of drawers next to his bed and rummaged through his riches.

"I have some gold, frankincense, and myrrh," he said. "They were leftover gifts from my brother's wedding. Which do you think best suits this occasion?"

"Why don't we bring all three?" said Imran. "Then each of us can give a gift, and they'll never know that we're regifting."

Prince Hamid placed the gifts in three small cloth sacks and tied them up with string. He gave the frankincense to Imran and the myrrh to Balbazaar. The men went to the stables, chose the best horses, and embarked on their journey.

Meanwhile, the days passed at The Butterfly Sanctuary with much commotion. King Herod had announced a census that required many Judeans to travel back to their cities of birth. Many such travelers arrived in Bethlehem with last-minute needs for lodging. As the rooms at the inn filled up, Abrahamus made sure to keep the best one vacant, knowing the promise he had made to Ezekliana and the Lord.

On the day he expected the travelers to arrive, Abrahamus went to the room to prepare it for his guests. Much to his surprise, stretched out on the bed lay Lucius, a young Roman bureaucrat and a regular at The Butterfly Sanctuary. He was short and flimsy, with a body that was tight and compact in every place except for his especially round bottom. He talked with a heavy lisp and walked with a womanly gait.

In modern parlance, he was a twink.

Lucius looked up at Abrahamus and grinned. "Hello there, Abrahamus," he said with a wink. "How are you doing?"

Abrahamus frowned. "What are you doing here?"

"Oh, I was in the area for work and wanted a place to stay for a few days. Dinah already checked me in."

Abrahamus shook his head. "This room is reserved for someone else. You will have to leave."

"For who?" Lucius asked rhetorically, and he gestured around the room. "I don't see anybody else here. And how does someone reserve a room in advance at an establishment like this one? Did they send you a messenger pigeon to inform you of their arrival?"

"No, an angel told me to make a reservation."

Lucius laughed and got up from the bed. He strutted over to Abrahamus and placed his hands on his chest. Abrahamus flinched.

"But what if I'm an angel," Lucius said, a sparkle in his eye, "and I'm asking for this room, too? Is there anything that I can do to convince you to let me stay? Perhaps I can do something to help alleviate your existing...reservations...?"

Lucius reached up and grasped Abrahamus's broad shoulders, and Abrahamus looked away, ashamed.

"No," he said, embarrassed, for he could feel his appendage growing harder as Lucius rubbed his shoulders. "There is nothing you can do."

Lucius pouted. "Are you really going to throw me out into the streets? I thought we had a special connection?"

Abrahamus winced. He knew what Lucius meant, and it made him feel even more ashamed. Although he had never acknowledged his feelings, Abrahamus had felt carnal desires for Lucius. The bureaucrat always behaved so libidinously with other men at the inn. A part of him admired such openness, but a part of him also resented it. He sometimes felt a jealous frustration with Lucius and his willingness to do as he pleased. Abrahamus fantasized about taking him face down in one of the cots, grabbing his bodacious rear and finding a way inside him. He imagined Lucius would groan with pleasure, the two of them giving in to the tension they always felt but that Abrahamus could never admit, for his shame was too great.

Lucius could sense that something troubled Abrahamus. He removed his hands and backed away.

"I'm just joking around, you know," Lucius said, his voice suddenly dropping an octave to sound decidedly heterosexual. "There's nothing wrong with a little joke between friends, right?"

It was only then, for the first time, that Abrahamus felt he had done something wrong. Here was Lucius, an attractive young man who had only ever been kind to him, and yet for some reason, inspired feelings of animus. And after Abrahamus had shown his discomfort, Lucius had changed his entire persona to make him feel more comfortable. The transformation reminded Abrahamus of how often he hid his feelings for men, how he never revealed his full, true self.

For a moment, he wondered if maybe he was wrong for pushing Lucius away. Perhaps, instead, he should be grateful for Lucius's openness and consider him a blessing. The Roman man showed him and others how men with aberrant desires can broadcast their truth to the world and still live a happy life full of joy.

But just as suddenly, Abrahamus pushed these thoughts away: no, his feelings were wrong! And while Lucius might misbehave openly, Abrahamus feared the consequences of such affections.

"I know you are joking," Abrahamus said, forcing a smile, and as he said the words, he felt an immeasurable amount of guilt. He felt the pain of lying, plus another layer of shame for the obvious truth: Lucius knew he was lying, too.

But lying was the only way that Abrahamus knew how to live.

"You can stay in this room," Abrahamus continued. "If the other travelers come, I will find another place for them."

He then closed the door and left.

All alone in his room, Lucius wondered about Abrahamus. Was he misreading all the cues he had seen over the years? Didn't Abrahamus share his desires?

Lucius had grown up in a well-to-do family in Rome, a city where men must maintain a façade of strength and masculinity. However, covertly, many of those same men engaged in indulgences with one another in private rooms, at bathhouses, and outside the city walls.

When he was 18, Lucius had discovered a group of young men with much openness about their behavior. The men taught him well, and over time, he gained confidence, believing that anything that gave him pleasure was good, no matter what others thought.

As he grew older, he resolved to seek out pleasures from around the world. He took a job as a bureaucrat that gave him plenty of opportunities to travel. On one of his trips to Judea, he delighted in meeting Dinah and Lara and discovering The Butterfly Sanctuary. It was the first of many visits. During his stays, he associated quite intimately with many of the other guests, but he had always eyed Abrahamus with so many questions. Abrahamus looked at him and some of the other more attractive lodgers with a funny expression: intrigued, yet detached, as if he were watching from miles away. Who was this attractive gentleman, and why did he remain so aloof?

Lucius wished he could sit Abrahamus down and have a proper conversation with him—ask him about his family, his upbringing—and serve as a gay mentor, much as the men in Rome had helped him. He wished he could help him achieve self-acceptance, no matter how arduous the journey might be.

He laid back down on his bed and sighed. Perhaps someday, someone special could help Abrahamus find happiness. Until that day came, he would admire Abrahamus from afar and gossip about him with the other guests at The Butterfly Sanctuary.

Dusk turned to evening, and soon, night had fallen. Abrahamus waited dutifully for the arrival of the travelers, but they did not appear until late in the night.

A knock came at the door, and when he answered, Abrahamus found a young man, a woman, and a mule that carried their belongings. Much to Abrahamus's surprise, the woman was very visibly pregnant, with a bulging belly that could fit a cask of wine.

"My good sir," the man said. "Please, tell me you have a place for us to stay! We traveled here for the census from very far away, but all the inns are full! There is nowhere for us to sleep!"

Abrahamus studied the weary travelers. They looked tired, and the woman dripped with sweat. He feared he had made a grave mistake in letting Lucius take the last room.

"I am sorry. All our rooms are full. But because of the census, I have set up two temporary beds in our stables. If you have no objection, you can sleep there tonight."

The man dropped to his knees and wept.

"Thank you, sir!" he cried out. "I cannot thank you enough. We have gone from inn to inn in this town, desperately seeking a room, praying for a place where my wife could rest. But we have been denied every time, until now. Thank you. Thank you. Thank you."

Abrahamus assured the man there was no need for such adulation and welcomed them into the inn. Their names, of course, were Joseph and Mary, and they had come from Nazareth in Galilee. He guided the couple to the stables, where he had used hay and spare tables from the courtyard to make two comfortable lofts. After giving them blankets, Abrahamus retired to his room.

The night was dark and full of stars, and as Abrahamus gazed up at them through his window, he wondered if his makeshift lodgings had satisfied the Lord. One star, directly above them in the sky, shone especially brightly. Abrahamus wondered if the star might be a sign, a message from the Lord saying yes, he had done his best, and the Lord was grateful to him.

Abrahamus crawled into bed and tried to fall asleep. But two hours later, he was awakened by a noise: the sound of a woman yelling, as though she might be giving birth…

Late in the night, Imran, Balbazaar, and Prince Hamid approached the gates of the city of Bethlehem. They dutifully followed the brightest star, just as Ezekliana had commanded. At a slow trot, their horses guided them to The Butterfly Sanctuary, where they heard the yelps of a woman coming from behind the inn. The men rode around to the stables in the back, where they found Joseph attending to Mary, in the midst of labor, her baby on the verge of birth.

"Good heavens!" Prince Hamid exclaimed. "The child is being born!"

Without giving it a second thought, Hamid dismounted from his horse and knelt next to Mary, holding her hand as she pushed.

"A doctor!" the prince called out to his friends, "One of you must go find a doctor!"

Right then, Abrahamus appeared. He saw Mary lying in the hay, struggling as she pushed. By instinct, he ran to help her.

"The baby is coming!" Joseph yelled. "Someone must help the baby!"

Abrahamus placed his hands down by the baby's legs, which had emerged from under Mary's night clothes. With a final push, the baby fell into Abrahamus's hands, its eyes wide and full of wonder. The newborn smiled and gazed up at Abrahamus admiringly.

Prince Hamid pulled out his knife and cut the umbilical cord.

"It's a boy," he declared.

Abrahamus looked up from the baby in his arms to see the man standing across from him—a man he recognized.

He froze.

The mysterious traveler stood before him, the one he had met only once so long ago but whose beautiful face had lingered with him for years. The man whose handsomeness had sent him down a path of shame and guilt, who had occupied his thoughts and tested his passions for so many nights, had appeared out of nowhere, dressed in tight pants that showed his shapely ass. His elegant, silk purple shirt was partially unbuttoned, flowing gracefully in the moonlight to reveal his smooth, tan skin, his bare chest, the curves of his hips, exuding all the same passions that had infected Abrahamus years ago and forever changed his life.

And Prince Hamid gazed back at Abrahamus, with a look of recognition, too. He had seen this man somewhere before, although he could not say where. The man had eyes that enchanted his soul, broad lips that called for a kiss, and wavy curls in his hair, the type he often loved to run his hands through. Had they not met once, many years ago, when they were both younger men?

Yes, Hamid recalled, this man had been sorting dates on a farm along a road he once took from Hebron to Jerusalem. He had noticed his boyish charm back then—but this man was no longer boyish! No, he was strong, tall, and muscular, with the domineering presence that Prince Hamid always found appealing. Immediately, he knew he wanted to connect with this man even more.

Joseph reached over and extracted the baby from Abrahamus's arms.

"Thank you, kind sirs, for your help," he said. "Can one of you bring my wife some water? She needs to drink, and we need to wash the baby."

Abrahamus snapped back to attention. "Yes," he said. "I can get water and cloths to wrap the baby."

He glanced over at Prince Hamid. At that moment, he recalled his thoughts from earlier in the day, during his conversation with Lucius, and the guilt he felt for pushing him away.

The appearance of his long-lost crush could not be a coincidence. Tonight, Abrahamus thought, he must take a chance and change his ways.

"Sir," he asked Prince Hamid, "can you help me fetch some water?"

Prince Hamid smiled.

"Certainly," he replied.

Imran and Balbazaar stood aside and silently watched their friend slip off with the hunky gentleman, both of them knowing they were powerless to stop any dalliance that might occur.

As Mary and Joseph tended to the baby, Abrahamus and Prince Hamid walked toward the inn. The two men closely followed one another, both of them aroused with tension and excitement. A joyous gift awaited them, indeed...

Interlude

Daddy Santa paused his story. He glanced down at the cute elf who lay in his arms and had been listening attentively for the past hour.

"Well, Tybel," Daddy Santa asked, "what do you make of the story so far?"

"Oh, I don't know, Santa," Tybel replied. "I do like it. I like it very much. But…"

Tybel hesitated, seemingly scared to speak.

"But what?" Santa insisted. "Is something wrong?"

"No, nothing is wrong. I just have a few questions about the historical accuracy of this story."

Daddy Santa frowned. "What do you mean?"

Tybel inhaled a deep breath before speaking:

"Well, in the Bible, doesn't Matthew 2:1-12 say that the wise men arrived in Bethlehem *after* Jesus's birth, so Prince Hamid could not have been present when he was born? And doesn't the Bible also say the wise men spotted a star in the East themselves and followed it without any reference to a visit from an angel? And didn't date farming only happen in specific regions of Judea in the 1st century B.C. that were far away from the areas around Bethlehem? And didn't the pitting of dates as a part of the cultivation process not begin as a consistent practice until more modern times? And weren't most buildings in Biblical times in Judea only one-story, making a two-story inn with a courtyard very unlikely? And don't many Biblical scholars believe that Mary and Joseph did not stay in a stable as we think of it in modern terms but more likely a cave, as that is where many animals were kept at the time? And weren't comforters not widely used in Europe and the Middle East until at least the 15th century, making their presence in each room at The Butterfly Sanctuary quite unlikely? And even though silk did exist in ancient China, didn't it not reach Europe until the 6th century A.D., making it extremely unlikely that Prince Hamid would have silk garments in his wardrobe? And even though fountains might have been invented and used in ancient Rome, isn't it even more unlikely that an inn in the outer reaches of the empire and managed by two widows and a destitute marginalized gay man would have the resources to own and maintain a fountain? And didn't men in ancient Greece and Rome most often use olive oil as a sexual lubricant, meaning men as wealthy as Prince Hamid would not typically resort to saliva? And isn't the idea of regifting as a social taboo a recent concept that was only first popularized in an episode of a sitcom in the 1990s? And since modern understandings of human sexuality were not developed until the 20th century, wouldn't an inn focusing on helping youths abandoned for being LGBTQ+ not necessarily identify itself as serving that particular population, but rather banished sinners more generally? And wouldn't such an inn then take in outcast youths who committed criminal or even violent acts, thus rendering The Butterfly Sanctuary an inherently unsafe environment?"

Daddy Santa squinted and scowled at the pesky elf who asked too many questions. Any semblance of his jolliness vanished, for Daddy Santa had his limits. He did not take kindly to criticism.

"Tybel," he said. "You're being naughty. What gives you the right to question the historical accuracy of this story—a treasured story passed down by gay men for many centuries?"

Tybel buried himself in Daddy Santa's thick, white chest hair.

"I'm sorry, Santa," he said. "I was just asking questions! Please, forgive me!"

"No," Daddy Santa said. "I won't forgive you so easily. You've been very, very naughty."

Sensing an opportunity, Tybel looked up at his lover.

"Well, if I am so naughty, doesn't that mean I need to be punished?"

Daddy Santa smirked.

"Are you saying what I think you're saying?"

Tybel nodded.

"Well then, how should I punish you?" Daddy Santa asked.

"Oh, I don't know. Maybe you should give me a *taste* of the punishment that you think I deserve..."

Tybel blushed at his unsubtle insinuation. His hand skimmed the inside of his lover's thigh.

Daddy Santa reacted to the signal swiftly.

He pushed Tybel off his chest and pinned him down on the bed. He then straddled the elf, unzipped his red pants, and placed his massive toy in front of Tybel's face. Soft at the moment, the long toy curved at the end, almost forming the shape of a candy cane.

Daddy Santa glowered down at Tybel.

"I think you owe me some penance. And clearly, I need you to stop asking me so many foolish questions. So, tell me: what's the best way for you to give me penance and keep yourself quiet?"

Tybel eyed Daddy Santa's large toy, enchanted by its prowess.

"Well, what are you waiting for?" Daddy Santa asked. "You know what to do."

Tybel smiled.

He knew exactly what Daddy Santa wanted.

And it was the same thing that Tybel wanted, too.

Slowly, Tybel leaned forward and put his mouth around Daddy Santa's toy, causing it to harden.

Daddy Santa placed his hand behind Tybel's head and pushed him forward.

"Very nice," Daddy Santa said, leaning forward to help fit the toy down Tybel's throat. "Give me penance for your sin."

Tybel arched his back and stared up at the beefy, bearded old man and the white body hair that ran down to his thighs. He reached up and massaged the man's belly.

"Oh yeah, that's perfect," Daddy Santa said with a sneer. "You're going to stay like this until I'm done. Now, where was I?"

As Tybel continued to moisten Daddy Santa, Daddy Santa proceeded with the rest of this story…

The Shepherds

The same night as the birth of Jesus, two shepherds watched over their flocks of sheep in the fields outside Bethlehem. An angel then appeared to them and told them about the new messiah. The official account of their story is well documented in Luke 2:8-20. However, some readers might wonder: why were these shepherds out in a field in the middle of the night, when their sheep were likely asleep? Why were they not resting in a tent or in a nearby shelter?

The answer is simple: they were copulating.

Jeremiah had a longstanding fetish for outdoor activities. In his many years as a shepherd, he had pursued every opportunity to explore the bodies of other willing shepherds while out in the fields. As the sheep slept, the shepherds took advantage of the dark of night to engage in deviant and pleasurable acts.

On this particular evening, after performing their duties to each other, Jeremiah lay on a blanket with his compatriot Levi, gazing up at the stars, the two of them entirely nude. It was a chilly night in the fields, but together, they kept each other warm. Levi rested one arm on Jeremiah's chest, and used his other arm to reach down and gently stroke the recently softened stick of his partner.

"Oh, Jeremiah," Levi said. "Are these stars not beautiful?"

"Yes," Jeremiah replied. "The stars are the most beautiful thing in the world…except for you, of course."

Levi snorted at the corniness of his comment.

"Wouldn't it be nice to lie in this pasture together forever, and no longer worry about sheep?"

Jeremiah quietly bristled at this notion, for he was not interested in commitment, and he did, in fact, enjoy being a shepherd. But he did not want to disturb Levi, a sweet young man who was new to this career. As a 22-year-old, Levi only had a few brown wisps of facial hair. And yet Levi, like Jeremiah, was tall, burly, and a little bit chubby, both of them covered with brown body hair.

In modern parlance, they were bears, and Jeremiah suspected that Levi might make a suitable cub.

At this moment, an orb of bright light appeared. Once again, it was Ezekliana. Upon seeing the naked shepherds, they rolled their eyes.

"Oh, for crying out loud!" Ezekliana shouted. "Why do I always have the worst timing? I keep manifesting before mortals just after they've engaged in intercourse!"

Embarrassed, Levi grabbed his side of the blanket and threw it over his private regions, his face turning red with shame. But Jeremiah did nothing to hide himself, for the apparition suited his exhibitionist inclinations. He grinned and continued to display his full self to Ezekliana.

"Hark, spirit!" Jeremiah cried out to the angel. "What brings you here to see our naked bodies?"

"I can assure you that my appearance has nothing to do with your nakedness," Ezekliana spat back. "I am an angel of the Lord, not a voyeur. And I am here to tell you of good nudes—err, sorry, good news!"

"Ah hah!" Jeremiah bellowed. "You said nudes!"

Ezekliana scowled. "You know what I meant! It was a Freudian slip—although, I suppose nobody shall use that term for at least another 1,900 years!"

Jeremiah shook his head and laughed. "You speak such nonsense, angel. Well, tell us, what is your good news?"

In all their millennia of serving as an angel of the Lord, Ezekliana had encountered all types of humans. They had seen the sad and forlorn, the joyous and humble, the prickly and irritated. But no human had so enraged Ezekliana as this nudist shepherd whose irreverent nonchalance got under their skin. They bit their lip and calmly continued.

"Behold! A child has been born in the stables of the inn you know as The Butterfly Sanctuary, down in Bethlehem. The Lord gives you this news so you can go spread the word, for this child is the son of God."

Levi hid under his blanket, but Jeremiah sat up slightly, leaning back on his elbows.

"Nice," Jeremiah said.

Ezekliana snapped. Their face turned pink with rage.

"That's it?" they yelled. "That's all you have to say to a child of the Lord being born in your city? God gives you his one and only son, and all you say is 'Nice'?"

Jeremiah, who typically stayed calm even when wolves approached his flock, sensed the angel's aggravation and started to panic. He sputtered: "I mean no offense, dearest spirit—"

"I am *not* a spirit!" Ezekliana cried out, and their orb of white light turned orange, before suddenly transforming into of a flaming, red ball of fire. "*I am an angel of the Lord!* And you shall recognize me as such!"

"Yes, yes, dear angel," Jeremiah stammered. "You are a great and lovely angel!"

Levi hid under the blanket in shame as Jeremiah attempted damage control.

"Please, dearest angel, tell me what I can do to make up for my mistakes. I meant no offense, and we both recognize your greatness, and the greatness of the Lord. We are meek and humble shepherds who enjoy spending time together in the fields, and we only wish to make you happy."

Ezekliana unclenched their fists. Gradually, the red ball of fire reverted back into the harmonious, shimmering white orb.

"Thank you," they replied. "To make up for your indiscretions, you must go see this child at once. And afterward, you must spread the good news to others, for that is the Lord's will."

Jeremiah bowed his head. "We shall do so, sweet angel."

By the time Jeremiah raised his head, Ezekliana had vanished into the starry night sky. Levi emerged from under the blanket.

"That was terrifying!" Levi shouted, still shaking, for his anxiety was only starting to ease. "I never want to upset an angel again!"

"Me neither," Jeremiah agreed. "We must go to Bethlehem at once to see this child, or else we might face this angel's wrath."

The shepherds packed up their belongings, put on their robes, and hurried to The Butterfly Sanctuary.

Back at the inn, Abrahamus guided Prince Hamid to the well in the courtyard. He asked him to retrieve water while he found some cloths to wrap the baby. As he entered the inn, his mind raced. Seeing Hamid was a great shock, but he also felt an intensifying warmth in his chest, as well as a tingling arousal in his manhood.

In the courtyard, a cool breeze blew through the air. Prince Hamid lowered the bucket into the well and filled it with water. He pulled the rope to raise the bucket, but as the bucket neared the top, it became stuck. He tugged on the rope, but for some reason, it would not move. Finally, he tugged so hard that the bucket shot upwards, flying out of the well and drenching him with water.

Abrahamus returned to the courtyard carrying a stack of cloths, only to find Hamid dripping wet, with drops of water shimmering in the starlight. The soaked purple shirt clung to the muscles of his body.

Abrahamus ran to the prince and set the cloths on the rim of the well.

"Oh heavens! I am so sorry. Here, let me help you."

He reached under Prince Hamid's shirt and peeled it off, revealing the prince's slim physique and his smooth, wet skin. An excitement stirred in Abrahamus as his hands touched the man, but then he stepped back, still too afraid to stand close to his long-lost flame.

Hamid took one of the cloths and rubbed it across his body, then began to pat his torso dry.

Abrahamus studied Hamid as he dried himself. He wondered if the man was an illusion, or maybe another angel sent to toy with his mind. But no, Hamid was real, standing before of him, half-naked: his flat stomach with well-defined abdominals, his firm yet delicate arms. He felt a burning desire to wrap himself around the man's wet body, but he was still working as an innkeeper. Such behavior would be unprofessional. Instead, he walked over to the well and retrieved some more water, which he poured into a clay jug.

As he finished toweling off, Prince Hamid looked over at Abrahamus.

"Here I am taking my clothes off in front of you, and I don't even know your name. Tell me, sir, who are you?"

Abrahamus shivered. He stepped back from the well and turned to face the prince.

"I am Abrahamus," he said, extending his hand for a handshake. "I work here at this inn. Who might you be, sir?"

The hand before Prince Hamid was large, firm and calloused—the hand of a working man with admirable strength.

Hamid shook his hand and smiled.

"People don't usually ask me my name. They know me as Prince Hamid Abgarid, son of King Abgar Abgarid of Osroene."

Abrahamus blanched. With hesitation, he offered the prince a small bow.

"Forgive me, Prince, for not recognizing you" Abrahamus said. "It is an honor to meet you."

Hamid laughed. "Please, such formalities are not necessary. I am traveling in foreign lands."

Abrahamus nodded, but he could already feel his shame growing even stronger. All these years, his secret desires for this man had boiled within him, a longing that tormented him every night. With this new revelation, he saw the hard truth: his passions were foolish, misguided. He was completely inadequate for a prince. And even if Hamid was offering some flirtatious signals, he could never view himself as Hamid's equal. The divide in status was too great.

But Prince Hamid persisted.

"Do you have a shirt that I can wear, Abrahamus?" he asked, grinning.

Abrahamus shook his head, but that did not stop Prince Hamid. He looked at the shirt Abrahamus wore—a simple white garment sewn from a linen sack—and reached out to feel its material, pinching its sleeve.

"This is a nice shirt," he said with a devious smile. "Would you be so kind to let me wear it? You are a bigger man than me, and my small body feels so cold!"

Being a kind gentleman and still entranced by the beauty and power of the prince, Abrahamus obliged. He took off his shirt and handed it to the visitor, revealing the rippling muscles of his chest and torso, his large, round pectorals, and his own well-defined abdominals.

Prince Hamid raised his eyebrows.

"You have an impressive body," he said as he put on the shirt. "And this shirt smells very nice, too."

Abrahamus blushed.

"Thank you," he mumbled. He then pointed at the water jug. "Before we forget, we should deliver these supplies to our guests."

The two walked back to the stables and gave the water and cloths to the couple. Mary quenched her thirst and then washed and wrapped the baby. Abrahamus hovered beside her and offered help.

Imran and Balbazaar, who had been waiting patiently, noticed Prince Hamid's new clothing, and the absence of a shirt from the masculine, muscular man. Imran pulled the prince aside.

"Did you already liaison with that man?" he asked.

Prince Hamid chuckled. "Do not worry," he said. "I merely borrowed his shirt. We haven't done anything…yet."

"Is he interested?" Imran asked. He moved his hand down to guard his crotch. The mere thought of this hunk and the prince together aroused him.

"I'm not quite sure," Hamid replied.

He glanced at Abrahamus, who was filling a manger with hay so the child could sleep in it. Mary stood beside him, holding the baby in her arms.

"Does your child have a name?" Abrahamus asked her.

Mary nodded. "Jesus."

"That's a good name for a child," Abrahamus agreed, and he gestured toward Joseph. "Did his father choose it?"

Mary looked up at Abrahamus, confused.

"Joseph is not his father," she said. "I am still a virgin. His father is the Lord, for Jesus is the Messiah, the son of God, who the Lord sent to us. An angel told us so and said to name him Jesus."

Abrahamus paused, baffled. He politely nodded once again and wondered if he had taken in a couple who had gone mad.

But then Balbazaar stepped forward.

"Why yes, he is the son of God! An angel came to us and told us so. That is why we traveled so far to meet him …and also to find some other unspecified 'joy,' whatever that might mean."

Abrahamus trembled. He did not want to mention his own encounter with an angel. Doing so would require him to admit his failure to follow the Lord's command. Instead, he shifted on his feet nervously and clenched his hands.

Hamid watched this interaction, then faced Imran.

"He seems very sweet, and I swear, I met a man like him once before, when he was much younger and even more shy. I think he might be suppressing something. I want to know him better. I feel that tonight is not a coincidence—that God has led me back to him for a reason. If I stayed here with him tonight, could you and Balbazaar find your own sleeping arrangements?"

Imran sighed. It was so predictable! Even though he had promised not to leave his friends, Prince Hamid was already plotting to abandon them. But when Hamid felt a special connection with someone, he rarely let it go easily. And there was one benefit: often, these connections turned Hamid into the best version of himself. In the weeks and months that followed, he would express his love for others even more fervently. His passions fueled other passions, his intimacy snowballing and building, thus making any future encounters even more pleasurable.

"I don't want to stop you," Imran said. "But if you go off with this man, where might we sleep?"

At that very moment, Jeremiah and Levi appeared.

"Hark! It is true!" Levi cried out upon seeing the baby. "A child has been born, and he is the son of God!"

Mary and Joseph gasped, shocked that even more people had heard this same story.

"We were tending our fields," Jeremiah explained, "When an angel came to us and told of us of such good news…"

As Jeremiah recounted the events from earlier in the evening, Balbazaar watched the tall, buff, illustrious shepherd gesticulate passionately. When the story finished, he made eye contact with Jeremiah and winked at him. And Imran had made eye contact with Levi, too. Perhaps it was the magic of the evening. Perhaps it was the work of the Lord. Regardless, undeniably powerful connections were felt between all the gentlemen: Balbazaar and Jeremiah, Imran and Levi, Abrahamus and Prince Hamid.

Balbazaar walked over to Imran and Hamid.

"Perhaps we shall not worry about where to sleep tonight," Balbazaar whispered. "I sense we have each found potential suitors who might offer us lodging."

Prince Hamid nodded. "Let us make haste."

After introducing themselves to Joseph and Mary, the wise men presented their gifts of gold, myrrh, and frankincense to Baby Jesus. Imran and Balbazaar then approached the

40

shepherds, while Hamid approached Abrahamus, who stood shirtless and lost in his thoughts.

"Can we return to your well and fetch some more water?" Hamid asked. "I am feeling a little bit thirsty."

Without another word or question, Abrahamus led him back to the well. When they got there, Hamid stopped and faced Abrahamus, looking up at his large brown eyes.

"I meant to say before that you look familiar. We have met before, haven't we?"

"Yes," Abrahamus replied curtly. He feared the direction of the conversation.

"Where did we meet?" Hamid asked.

"At the farm where I grew up," Abrahamus said. "You came on horseback and asked me for directions."

Prince Hamid beamed with joy.

"So it was you!" he exclaimed. "I recognize you. You were the cute boy sorting dates on the road from Hebron."

Abrahamus raised his eyebrows. "Oh, you thought I was cute?"

Prince Hamid laughed, "Yes, I did."

Abrahamus laughed too, but then the wave of shame crashed back over him. He forced a grimace across his face and suppressed his laughter.

"Sorry," he said, and he turned his head away.

Hamid took a step toward Abrahamus and placed a hand on his thick, bulging forearm.

"Sorry for what?" Hamid asked.

Abrahamus looked back at Hamid and gazed into his beautiful green eyes. The prince seemed so comfortable as they stood next to each other. He felt a natural bond, as if this soft hand was always meant to grasp his hardened muscles.

And yet, Abrahamus had been told his whole life that such a connection was unforgiveable.

"I don't want to give you the wrong idea," he finally said.

Prince Hamid smirked. "The wrong idea about what?"

"That I might want you to feel something for me."

"Well, you do want me to feel something, don't you?"

Hamid playfully rubbed Abrahamus's forearm. Then he took his hand.

"You have very strong hands," Hamid said. "Do you have to grip things very hard when you work?"

"Yes," Abrahamus replied. "Sometimes."

Hamid stepped forward. His forehead touched Abrahamus's shoulders, and his chest pressed against the muscles in Abrahamus's abdomen. He guided Abrahamus's hand down and around his body, placing it on his butt.

"Show me how strong you can grip."

Abrahamus couldn't help himself. The shame melted away. He squeezed Hamid's butt hard, groping its firm shape with delight, and courageously, without giving it another thought, he leaned forward and kissed him on the lips.

They held the kiss for a few seconds of pure bliss. Then Abrahamus pulled back, smiling down at his beloved.

There was no guilt anymore.

There was no fear.

All he felt was love.

Hamid smiled back. "Wow," he said. "I'm impressed. You have tasty lips and a very strong grip."

"Is that what you want?" Abrahamus asked, his heart beating fast. "A man who can squeeze you hard?"

Hamid nodded and rested his head on Abrahamus's chest. "Nothing makes me feel better than feeling the touch of a man who makes me smile."

"Ah, so, I'm cute, and I make you smile?"

Hamid smirked again. "Oh, you could make me do more than just smile!"

And this time, Hamid reached back and pulled Abrahamus's hand away from his ass. He guided his hand around to the front of his body, down to his crotch, so Abrahamus could feel a hardened object of desire. It was surprisingly large, although not as large as Abrahamus's appendage, which was also bulging, the outline appearing through his own pants.

Hamid then reached forward and touched Abrahamus's bulge, stroking it slowly.

"Looks like I could make you do a few things, too."

Abrahamus didn't respond. He was too entranced by the prince's plump lips, his gentle touch. He leaned forward and kissed him again.

"I don't understand it," he admitted, "but you have an effect on me. It's a power beyond my control."

Hamid continued to stroke Abrahamus.

"Can we go somewhere with more privacy?" Hamid asked.

Abrahamus nodded. He took Hamid's hand and led him into the inn, up the stairs, and into his bedroom...

The Not-So-Silent Night

Prince Hamid had never seen such humble lodgings. The bedroom only had a cot and a candle, which Abrahamus had left lit, evoking a sensual ambiance. A window looked out upon the courtyard. Breathtaking stars sparkled in the night sky, shining light from the heavens and blessing the love between the two men.

Despite the bare room, Hamid felt comfort in its simplicity, for he already possessed the most valuable object of all: the object of his heart's desire. He sat on the bed and looked up at Abrahamus, who stood before the doorway.

The prince took off Abrahamus's shirt and handed it back to him.

"Thank you for letting me use your shirt," he said.

Abrahamus took the shirt and stepped toward Hamid.

"Do you not want to keep wearing it? The night can turn cold sometimes."

Hamid smiled.

"I'm hoping we can find other ways to stay warm."

Abrahamus gazed down at Hamid, his slim waist, his luscious lips, his elegant, long eyelashes. For years, he had fantasized about ravishing this beautiful young man with all his passion and love, of grabbing his waist, of kissing his lips…but as the man sat before him, Abrahamus stayed still. The thick muscles in his arms and chest quivered.

"Is something wrong?" Hamid asked, a pleading look in his eyes.

Abrahamus remained paralyzed, unsure how to move, how to approach the godlike soul before him. He took one step closer, and then he fell to his knees.

"Forgive me, Prince Hamid," he said. "I am not worthy."

Hamid laughed, believing Abrahamus to be joking. "What do you mean? How are you unworthy?"

Abrahamus looked up at Hamid, and suddenly it all became clear. He was a worshipper of this prince, and as a humble innkeeper, he must do as he was told.

Abrahamus bowed his head, the shame of a common man washing over him. "Please, sir, I do not know how any of this can be—how you came to be here in my room tonight. None of it makes sense."

"Why, it is fate, just as God intended," Hamid replied. "I followed the star in the sky to you, as the Lord's angel commanded."

But Abrahamus shook his head.

"I am the son of a date farmer. I live a quiet life and keep to myself. And I have brought neither a man nor a woman to this room before tonight."

A puzzled expression appeared on Hamid's face.

"You have never had a nighttime visitor? Ever?"

Abrahamus nodded, and his eyes began to water from the strong sense of shame.

A thought then occurred to Prince Hamid.

"Tell me, Abrahamus, how did you become an innkeeper here in Bethlehem? Did something happen between you and your family?"

Abrahamus looked up at Hamid. Tears ran down his cheeks.

"I was banished."

Hamid extended a hand to the innkeeper's cheek and wiped away his tears.

"Why would they banish a man as good and honest as you?"

Abrahamus turned his head away from Hamid.

"Because I am not good," he said, and he began to weep. "I have been afflicted with bad thoughts. Impure thoughts of men that I cannot control...beautiful men like you."

Upon hearing these words, Hamid's heart broke. He understood all too well what Abrahamus meant.

"And I have never told anyone of these thoughts before," Abrahamus continued. "Except my parents, who then exiled me. But these thoughts, they have continued to haunt me. I know I am not alone, and I know there are others who have feelings like mine...but I am scared. I am too afraid of what might happen if I ever were to reveal my desires. And it has made me feel so alone. So horribly alone!"

Abrahamus's head crashed to the floor, and he wept at Prince Hamid's feet.

At a moment like this, a lesser man might flee. The groveling, the emotion—it could all seem melodramatic and overbearing. But the kind-hearted man that was Prince Hamid only felt empathy for Abrahamus.

Hamid climbed off the bed, crouched down on the floor next to the man, and gently wrapped his arm around him, cradling this wounded soul. Together, they rocked back and forth.

"It's okay, it's okay," Hamid repeated in a hushed tone. "You are worthy, Abrahamus. You are more than worthy to me."

Slowly, Abrahamus calmed himself, his tears subsiding. He sat up on the floor next to Hamid and stared into his eyes.

"You are a beautiful and powerful man," Abrahamus said. "Why are you sitting on the floor here, wasting your time with me?"

"Because I see you, Abrahamus," Hamid replied, resting his hand on the man's cheek. "I see your beauty and your power. You are strong. You have integrity. And you speak from the heart. You are everything a man like me could want in a lover."

And Abrahamus could not hold back any longer. He leaned forward and kissed Prince Hamid, pushing him down to the floor. Hamid tipped his head back and lifted his body off the floor, offering all of himself to his lover. Abrahamus pushed his hands down Hamid's pants, grabbing his buttocks and pulling him up toward his body. They kissed passionately, their tongues in their mouths, their muscles flexed, their groins pulsing hard against each other.

Abrahamus leaned back and stared down at Prince Hamid. "How is this not a sin?" Abrahamus asked.

Prince Hamid placed a hand on Abrahamus's hard crotch.

"This is the love that the Lord has given us," he said. "If we are honest with one another, and if we treat each other with respect, then it can never be a sin."

Abrahamus hesitated, panting as he stared into Hamid's green eyes, as Hamid rubbed him and continued to talk.

"You have always felt this way, haven't you? The feelings you feel are a gift from the Lord. He has been generous with us and made us special. I know some are scared of how we're different from other men. I know that your parents, as good and hardworking as they might be, taught you to feel shame. But I have read the holy texts of many religions. And while some may discourage lust or greed, vanity or indulgences, no one ever speaks ill of love."

Hamid placed his hand around Abrahamus's head and pulled him in close.

"Whatever you think of me, whatever you think of yourself, know that there is no shame in the feelings the Lord gave us. For honest feelings are right and pure. I believe the Lord speaks through us—through our hearts and through our minds. You have my heart. You have my mind. You have my spirit and my soul."

Hamid kissed Abrahamus, and Abrahamus smiled.

"Are you saying, Prince Hamid, that the Lord commands me to be with you?"

He squeezed Hamid's butt, and Hamid laughed.

"Yes," he said. "And I command you, too."

In one motion, Abrahamus stood up and lifted Hamid off the floor. He pulled the prince close to his chest, carried him to his bed, and laid him down gently.

"Is this more comfortable?" he asked, settling next to him in the bed.

Hamid scooted close to Abrahamus's body and kissed him again.

"Now I am comfortable," he said.

They pulled off their pants, and Hamid cupped his palms around Abrahamus's large appendage and his dangling sack of jewels. The appendage stood erect, fully and gloriously.

"The Lord has given you a gift," Hamid said with a smile.

Abrahamus smiled back. "It's your gift now."

Hamid kissed the appendage, tickling it with his tongue, and Abrahamus fell back into a state of bliss. With his lips locked tightly around the shaft, Hamid slid down the full length. The girth filled his throat and his soul, until his lips touched the curly pubic hairs at the base. He looked up at Abrahamus, who gleamed down with pride at Hamid. His lips retraced the path up the shaft, and then quickly back down, up and down, up and down, racing back and forth rapidly, his lips pressing so tightly that he made Abrahamus throb.

"Oh Lord!" Abrahamus cried out in pleasure. "This is your gift! This is the greatest gift of all!"

He placed his hand behind Hamid's head, gently guiding him as the prince continued to copulate with this mouth.

Finally, Hamid pulled back. He licked the head of Abrahamus's appendage, covering it with saliva, then looked up at his partner. Abrahamus heaved deep breaths.

"You know," Prince Hamid said, "I have other gifts that I can share with you, too."

Before Abrahamus could say anything else, Hamid sat up and placed his ass on the hard appendage. He spit into his hand and rubbed his saliva in the appropriate places. Abrahamus watched in a state of wonder, still harder than he had ever been in his life—harder than the many nights when he had fantasized and rubbed his appendage ferociously, never believing any of his dreams could come true.

Hamid stared at Abrahamus with an earnest yearning, a passionate desire.

"I'm ready," he said, and he kissed Abrahamus's chest. "Do what you want with me."

A spirit awakened in Abrahamus. He flipped Hamid onto his side and pulled him close to his crotch, inserting himself. Hamid winced with delight at the pain of such a large appendage, which Abrahamus began thrusting, pushing himself harder and harder into the beautiful man in his bed. The tightness around his shaft rubbed his most sensual spots better than his hand ever could, and Hamid felt an immense force pushing against his most pleasurable place, again and again and again.

By instinct, Abrahamus moved his hand down to Hamid's erection, gripping it like a broom handle.

"I want you to feel it, too," Abrahamus said. "Do you feel it?"

"Yes," Hamid said.

"Do you feel good?"

"Yes!" he said louder.

"Do you want it harder?"

"Yes!" Hamid yelled, his face contorting with the Lord's long-promised joy.

Abrahamus gripped Hamid harder, thrusted his pelvis faster, rammed himself deeper, and Hamid moaned in a euphoria more vivid than any he had ever felt before, not even with the strongest and most adept soldiers of his kingdom, nor Imran, nor Balbazaar, nor the most talented concubines in the world. And Abrahamus was moved to give even more pleasure—to use his free hand to pinch Hamid's nipples, to lean forward and nibble on Hamid's ear, acts beyond his imagination but that the spirit compelled. He was compelled by the Lord to lift Hamid up onto his hands and knees, still inside him, still thrusting from behind, towering over him and grabbing him by the shoulders to pull him closer, his appendage reaching even deeper.

"Oh yes, Abrahamus! Don't stop!" Hamid begged. "Keep going! Keep going!"

Abrahamus obeyed, addicted to the passions that moved them both—a passion not rooted in carnal desires, but in love, the eagerness to commit to each other's happiness, to maximize their pleasure. Abrahamus leaned over and kissed Hamid's shoulders and neck, then pushed Hamid flat on the bed so he could ram himself fully inside.

In a burst of ecstasy, Abrahamus relieved himself, and Hamid did so into the bed sheets. Hamid clenched the cheeks of his butt, squeezing the remnants of the appendage's gooey gift, until Abrahamus withdrew himself and rolled over onto his back.

Hamid rested his head on his partner's shoulder and kissed his neck. Abrahamus began to cry again.

"That was...amazing," Abrahamus said, tears of joy falling down his face. "I have been waiting for such relief my whole life. You are beautiful—more beautiful than I ever imagined."

Hamid stroked his chest. "You amazed me, too. In all my years...I have never felt this way before. I have never felt so loved."

Cuddling together, the two men fell asleep. The stars in the sky still shone brightly, still blessing them and their bliss.

"There is no sin in our love," Abrahamus muttered.

Hamid placed a kiss on Abrahamus's right nipple.

"No," he whispered, "love as strong as this is a gift from God. It can never be a sin."

As the two lay together in silence, entangled with another, Abrahamus felt the desire to confess:

"Since we first met, so many years ago, I have been seeing you in my dreams. When my father first discovered my...attractions, and that I played with myself...it was you who I fantasized about. And every night since then, your memory, your beauty has stayed with me..."

The meaning of the words sunk into Hamid. He knew they were words some might fear—the obsessive ramblings of a sickened stalker, a lust that could drive a man mad. But lying with Abrahamus, he only felt peace and love.

The prince beamed with joy and kissed his partner's left nipple.

"I wish I had seen you in my dreams," he admitted. "But I never could have dreamed of a man as amazing, as humble, as incredible, as strong, or as glorious as you."

Abrahamus rubbed Hamid's back, and Hamid nuzzled Abrahamus's chest. The two men soon drifted off to sleep, both thankful that their dreams had come true.

The next morning, Abrahamus and Hamid slept in. When they eventually came downstairs to the courtyard, they found the guests abuzz with news that had spread: a child of the Lord had been born, a messiah meant to bring peace and joy to the world!

Joseph and Mary sat with Baby Jesus on the outer edges of the courtyard, not far from the stables, quietly keeping to themselves. None of the guests seemed to realize that this new messiah was staying with them at the inn, cooing in the arms of his mother, who rocked him gently.

Imran, Balbazaar, Jeremiah, and Levi sat at a table nearby, silently drinking some tea. Prince Hamid and Abrahamus approached them.

"Greetings, friends," Abrahamus said, his face glowing with joy. "How was the rest of your evening?"

The four men grinned at each other, all of them afraid to speak first.

"Well," Imran finally said, "We had a good night together. The four of us made another friend."

Prince Hamid raised his eyebrows. "Oh?" he asked. "And who was this friend?"

At that moment, Lucius emerged from the inn, his hair somewhat disheveled. He strutted over to the table.

"Hello, gentlemen," he said with a sultry smile. "How are you all feeling this morning?"

The four men seated at the table did not respond with words. Their gleeful expressions told the whole story.

Lucius glanced at Abrahamus and Hamid. He noticed how closely they stood together, how Abrahamus wrapped his arm around Prince Hamid's shoulder. Why, he had never seen

51

Abrahamus touch anyone before, let alone a male guest! He paused, and as the thought occurred to him, he gasped.

"I'm sorry, sir," he said, addressing Prince Hamid, "but are my eyes deceiving me? Did you spend the evening with this muscular man last night?"

Abrahamus blushed, but Hamid stood unembarrassed next to his partner. He placed his hand on Abrahamus's chest and patted him lovingly.

"He was a most honorable host," the prince said. "I'm delighted he offered me a bed."

"So was Lucius for us," Balbazaar said with a sly grin.

Abrahamus furrowed his eyebrows. "For all four of you? But, why, there is only one bed in his room! Did you all sleep on the floor?"

The four men at the table and Lucius exchanged looks with one another, unsure of what to say. They all thought back to the previous night, reminiscing on the salacious events that had transpired...

Not long after Abrahamus and Prince Hamid left the stables, the other men had wandered off together into an adjacent alley. They introduced themselves to each other, commended the miracle of Jesus's birth, and eventually acknowledged the arousals they felt for one another. Immediately, they began to make plans.

"I must admit," Balbazaar said, "This night is quite cold, and we are tired from a long journey. The two of you wouldn't happen to know of a place where we could sleep?"

Jeremiah looked at Levi nervously, and Levi looked back at him. Levi spoke first.

"I wish we could offer you both lodging suitable for men of your caliber, but regrettably, we are mere shepherds. At night, we prefer to tend to our flocks in the fields outside this city. We do not have a place to stay."

Imran and Balbazaar became crestfallen, their hopes for both sleep and indulgence having seemingly been dashed.

"When we tend our flocks at night, though, we make due," Jeremiah said. "We stay warm with blankets, and we often find time to engage in other...activities..."

Imran looked at Balbazaar nervously, and Balbazaar looked back at him. Imran spoke up.

"I don't think Balbazaar and I are fond of sleeping outdoors. Is there not some shelter in your field where we could warm each other up and sleep for the night?"

Levi shook his head. An awkward silence fell amongst the four men. Then Jeremiah snapped his fingers.

"Wait! We cannot sleep yet anyway, for the angel who visited us demanded we spread the news of Jesus's birth! For this one night, we must first devote ourselves to the Lord, before we can devote ourselves to each other."

"Huh?" Balbazaar said.

Jeremiah smiled at Balbazaar and slapped him on the back. "I'll tell you what, friend. Why don't we spend an hour or two spreading the news of Jesus's birth to others, see who we meet, and maybe doing so will lead us to shelter?"

Balbazaar looked at Imran. Imran looked at Levi. Levi shrugged.

"Why not?" Imran said. "It is what the angels want!"

As a pack, the four men walked the streets of Bethlehem. They approached any strangers and asked them if they had heard the good news: a messiah had been born, a son of God, who would bring peace to the Earth.

A few hours later, Lucius passed by on horseback. He was returning from a day in Jerusalem, where he had met with the leaders of the region to discuss important government business. The tall, handsome men bustling about the street captured his curiosity. He stopped, dismounted from his horse, and approached them.

"Pray tell," he asked in his distinctly effeminate voice, his hand on his hip in a most sassy pose, "What are you boys yelling about at such a late hour?"

The four men immediately recognized that this man might be a great asset. Despite his short stature and slim body, he stood with confidence and wore the garb of a government official. His amorous demeanor offered many implications. And as he stood before them, his purple toga blew in the night breeze, briefly exposing a round and supple bottom beneath his garments.

"Most excellent sir," Jeremiah said, "are you an official who holds a special status in this land?"

"Why, yes," Lucius replied. "I am here on official state business from Rome. But of course, I do not *only* travel for business. I *always* try to travel for both business *and* pleasure!"

The four men glanced at each other. They were all a bit shocked at the boldness of Lucius's advances. Seeing their astonishment, Lucius laughed.

"Come, gentlemen. Don't be shy. Tell me: how can I best serve you?"

"Well, we do need a place to sleep tonight," Imran replied. "But first, we are spreading the good news. Have you heard yet about the birth of our new savior, the son of God?"

Lucius raised his eyebrows. As an official who had voyaged across the Roman Empire, from Iberia to Egypt, he had occasionally encountered mad men and charlatans who claimed to possess divine powers. However, he had never heard of a baby claiming to be the son of God. He was intrigued.

"I have not heard this news," he replied. "Was this baby born in Bethlehem?"

"Why yes!" Levi answered. "He was born a few hours ago. An angel came to us shepherds in the fields this evening, and he told us of his birth."

"And an angel came to the two of us, too," Balbazaar added, gesturing to himself and Imran. "We are noblemen from Osroene, and only a few days ago, an angel visited us and told us of this child's coming birth. And lo and behold, we found him in the stables of an inn, just as predicted!"

"An inn?" Lucius asked. "Which inn is this savior at?"

"The Butterfly Sanctuary!" Levi replied.

Lucius's eyes widened. "That's where I am staying tonight! Come, take me to this messiah. I want to pay him my respects in person."

Lucius mounted his horse and followed the men to the stables. Mary and Joseph had fallen asleep, resting in the hay on the tables. The baby lay wrapped in cloths, sleeping quietly in the manger, a beam of light from a star in the sky shining down upon him.

When Lucius saw the child, a chill ran down his spine. He knew he should maintain skepticism of any claims of holiness—a government official giving credence to a new messiah might undermine the power of the state. But the starlight, the calm, the sense of tranquility all spoke to him, and he felt a desire to believe...a desire also fueled by a carnal craving to lure four handsome men back to his room!

"Yes," Lucius said, speaking with some hesitation, "this child could very well be the son of God!"

The men disregarded his tentativeness.

"Hark! He believes!" Balbazaar cried out, and he jumped in the air with joy.

Lucius nodded politely, and the four men simpered with pride, feeling confident they had sufficiently spread the good news of Jesus's birth.

"This miracle calls for a celebration," Lucius continued. "You mentioned needing a place to sleep. Perhaps you can all come to my room, where we can celebrate a little?"

The men eagerly followed Lucius to his room, where he closed the door and lit the candelabra. Lucius had left the window open, and the moon and the stars shone heavenly light onto his bed.

"So, my fellow travelers," Lucius said, "how do you propose we celebrate?"

Imran, Balbazaar, Levi, and Jeremiah all looked at each other nervously, unsure of what to say. They all felt aroused by Lucius and each other, but they did not know how to proceed.

"Oh, come on now!" Lucius said. He walked over to Jeremiah, pulled back the shepherd's robe, and placed his hand on his hairy chest. Lucius looked up at the tall, attractive shepherd, who smiled back at him. "Do *none* of you have any ideas for how we might celebrate?"

Levi began to sweat, for he always felt anxious in unpredictable situations. "Maybe we could open a bottle of wine. Do you have any?"

"I'm afraid not," Lucius said as he approached the other shepherd. He rested his arms on Levi's shoulders, then traced his hands down his body. "I wonder, though, if any of you gentlemen might have any big bottles of your own that I could drink from tonight?"

Balbazaar, who had finally caught on to the innuendos, began to fondle himself. Imran, feeling brave, stepped forward and placed a hand on Lucius's shoulder.

"It sounds like you are asking us to give you something. But maybe you should first show us what gifts you can offer in return?"

Lucius smirked. He strode over to the bed and climbed on top of it, standing before the men in his room.

"Perhaps you gentlemen would like to preview the festivities I have planned for this evening," he said.

Slowly, he reached back and untied his toga, allowing it to reveal his lithe body and his shaved chest. As he let the toga descend, he revealed to his guests a slim, sculpted stomach, with a six pack of abdominals that sat above his perfect V-line, his nimble hips. He then revealed a posterior as large and round as a watermelon. His skin was smooth and flawless—no pimples, no stretch marks, and no hair anywhere, for he shaved religiously. As his toga dipped lower, Lucius revealed his genitals—not too big, not too small, and just the right size to fit in a burly man's hands—and thick, strong calves that glistened in the moonlight. Lucius slipped off his sandals and let the toga fall past his feet, displaying his naked body to the four suitors. Their mouths hung open, and their own bodies had hardened underneath their robes.

"Amazing," Balbazaar said, continuing to fondle himself.

Lucius stepped off the bed and sashayed back over to Imran. He placed his hands on his shoulders.

"Well, gentlemen," he said, turning to look toward all the men, "would you like to join me in my bed tonight? I would hate for anyone to sleep on their own..."

Imran could not resist the opportunity. He leaned forward and kissed the man on his forehead...and then his nose...and then his lips.

"It would be an honor," he said, "to share a man as beautiful as you."

As Imran began to massage Lucius's round buttocks, Jeremian approached Lucius from behind. He reached around to grab the twink by the hips, pressing his groin against Lucius's behind so that he also felt the soothing motion of Imran's hands. Jeremiah leaned down and kissed Lucius on the neck.

"I, too, would be honored," Jeremiah said, "to partake in an evening in which you are shared."

And then Jeremiah looked up at Imran, whose eyes glimmered with pleasure. The two men leaned forward and shared a kiss, with Lucius standing between them. Lucius watched from below and smiled seductively.

"Oh my," he said. "This evening has taken yet another unexpected turn!"

Levi, still trembling with nervousness, stepped forward and kneeled before the three men.

"Please, sir," he said, looking up at Lucius. "I want to make sure that you are pleasured, too. May I?"

Lucius nodded knowingly, and Levi locked his lips around the modest shaft that hung between the man's legs.

Balbazaar continued to fondle himself in the corner, his hand reaching under his robe.

"Don't worry about me," he told the other men. "I prefer to watch."

Lucius winked at him. "If you change your mind, let us know."

The men moved to the bed, where Imran claimed Lucius's mouth, Jeremiah advanced on his posterior, and Levi tasted his most precious parts. The men moved in unison, with Lucius commanding them as a conductor leads a symphony, gyrating to a rhythm that the others followed. His hands touched their bodies most sensually, his fingers gliding across their muscular arms, chests, backs, and legs, feeling them as they flexed and moved with passion, then moved faster and faster as they tightened around one another, panting and sweating as they crescendoed toward their climaxes.

Balbazaar stood at the corner of the bed, his robe having fallen to the floor, and he rubbed himself with great fervor, his erection standing large before the group.

"My Lord, I'm about to erupt!" he cried out jubilantly.

But the men were too focused on one another to notice— not even when Balbazaar's white substance flew through the air and landed on their arms, their legs, and Lucius's cheeks, which Levi sat up to lick. Imran removed himself from Lucius to let Levi clean the face, which led Levi to Lucius's mouth. As the two kissed and tongued one another, Balbazaar's offering swished back and forth between them until, finally, they both swallowed.

"The man tastes like a fruit of the Gods," Lucius said.

Imran, who had started to rub himself aggressively as Levi and Lucius kissed, then exploded too, his ejaculate falling onto both their faces. Eagerly, the men repeated their routine, gleefully accepting Imran's offering.

"I only have one question now," Levi said, as he kissed Lucius's chest and moved down his body. "Do you taste as good as the noblemen?"

And Levi resumed his work on Lucius's crotch, rubbing himself as he did, while Jeremiah continued to work on his behind, pounding away until he climaxed, too.

"Only two of us left now," Lucius said, looking down at Levi's pretty hazel eyes. He playfully stroked the shepherd's chin. "Who will finish first?"

The answer was neither of them, for they finished at the same time, when Lucius reached down and pinched Levi's nipples. The two men fell beside each other, exhausted.

"Don't tell any of the others," Levi whispered to Lucius, "But you tasted the best to me!"

Lucius giggled, and the three other men, who rested on the floor by the bed, sat up.

"What's so funny?" Balbazaar asked.

Lucius shook his head, "Oh, nothing. I just find it remarkable how lovely this holy night has been. All that has transpired…why, it has felt like a dream, or a conspiracy of the Gods."

Jeremiah climbed up onto the bed and kissed Lucius on the lips. "It is a joyous night, indeed," he agreed.

Lucius waved Imran and Balbazaar back over to the bed.

"Come, join us. We should all sleep together in the bed tonight, so that we can stay warm. And who knows…maybe we will find inspiration again later in the evening…"

Imran and Balbazaar squeezed in next to Lucius, Levi, and Jeremiah, the five of them embracing each other, all of them thankful that the Lord had brought them together…

In the courtyard the next day, following Abrahamus's inquiry about their sleeping arrangements, the five men hesitated, unsure of how many details they should divulge.

"Perhaps we should leave our nighttime activities to the night," Jeremiah finally said. "Although, we did not spend the whole night in the room. In fact, we spent much of last night spreading the good news of Jesus's birth, just as the angel requested."

"Is that so?" Hamid asked.

"Yes," Imran said, "And now, the whole town of Bethlehem is talking about the new messiah!"

Lucius smiled at the enthusiasm of Imran—an enthusiasm he felt deeply last night and greatly appreciated.

"While I would love to talk more," he said, "I'm afraid that I must leave for work. I am due to see King Herod in Jerusalem."

"Oh, good!" Balbazaar said. "Can you spread the good news of Jesus's birth to the king?"

Lucius paused.

"I am not sure if that is the best idea," he said. "But I will mention the news if it seems appropriate."

"Why not?" Balbazaar asked, confused. "Wouldn't a king want to know about the birth of the son of God?"

Lucius sighed. "He probably would want to know this news. But with *this* king, discretion might be advisable."

Lucius hurried toward the stables to retrieve his horse, with thoughts of the political implications of Jesus's birth weighing heavily on his mind...

The Mad Queen and the Escape

For many reasons, Abrahamus was lucky to have found Prince Hamid. He had found love, purpose, and his soulmate, but the prince had also prevented him from wandering down a dark path that those in the closet sometimes follow. It is a sad truth that the heavens know too well, and that we have seen play out repeatedly throughout history: when a gay man denies the sexuality that God gave him, he can suffer in silence and let evil seep into his soul. He can turn vain, lashing out at those he believes to be more joyful than him, blaming others for his woes and frustrations.

In Judea, no greater example of this phenomenon existed than King Herod, a man whose outlandish flamboyance has been overlooked by many straitlaced, heterosexual historians. He had forty different varieties of pink and purple togas, which he switched between throughout each day to suit his varying moods. During his reign, he demanded the construction of many large and unnecessarily phallic monuments, commissioned garish murals, bought tacky vases, jewelry, and other finery, which he left strewn about his quarters hap hazardously. He had a team of fifty servants, all men between the ages of 18 and 29, for he would dismiss any servant whose lack of youth made him feel old. He would regularly dismiss servants for petty reasons, too, little grievances or mistakes for which he showed no grace. Sometimes, he would even execute them. His palace therefore had a notoriously high turnover rate, and only the most desperate would dare to work for him.

He had multiple marriages and wives, none of whom he satisfied, for his attractions were exclusively kept for another gender. But because he refused to accept his sexual orientation, he blamed his wives for the failures of his marriages, shunned them, and inevitably repeated the cycle with a new woman. Although some of these wives bore him children, all were from liaisons with other men. King Herod would play dumb and take credit for their seeds.

And as King Herod slept at night, always avoiding interaction with the woman in his bed, he would think of his fairest male servants and pine for them. He never acted on these feelings, for he felt deep insecurity over how he might be perceived—weak, feminine, unmanly.

Instead of confronting his truth, he stewed in rage over his unattainable desires, with jealousy for the wives and girlfriends of his servants. Come the morning, this jealousy would seep into his governance. He snapped at guards for imperfect posture. He threw tantrums over minor offenses by subjects within the kingdom. He imprisoned or even executed those who might challenge his authority.

In his time, he was known as a vicious and cruel tyrant. But in modern parlance, King Herod was a mad, bitchy, messy, toxic, closet case of a queen.

Because of the rumors of disturbances in King Herod's palace, Roman officials had dispatched one of their finest civil servants, Lucius, to observe the social dynamics of the regional government. He was tasked with determining if diplomatic measures could alleviate any tensions.

After only a few days in Judea, Lucius had decided that there simply was no hope: King Herod was unhinged, and the palace's problems were fully attributable to the ruler. He intended to write a full report for his superiors when he returned to Rome. Until then, he could only observe palace activities and document the atrocities.

On the day after Jesus's birth, Lucius discovered quite a scene. The palace was an enormous, ostentatious building, plastered with gaudy frescos depicting King Herod achieving many physical feats: running, wrestling, pole vaulting, swimming. Steps led up to the main entrance, with giant columns standing on either side. The shards of three broken vases rested in this entryway, and a young servant lay against the right column, crying.

Lucius approached the man and squatted next to him.

"My good sir, what happened here this morning?"

The young man wiped the tears from his eyes.

"King Herod threw another fit," he said. "He screamed at us because his tea was not hot enough this morning. But just yesterday, he had screamed at us because his tea was too cold..."

Lucius shook his head, aghast.

"Tell me, what do you think bothers this man so greatly? Why does he always rage?"

The servant shook his head.

"We don't know. But this morning, he yelled at a messenger about somebody named Jesus. Whoever Jesus is, he seemed especially mad at him today."

Lucius closed his eyes and placed his hand on his forehead. He had hoped the news of Jesus's birth might not arrive in Jerusalem so soon. But alas, gossip spread fast in Judea.

"Collect yourself and return to your duties," Lucius told the servant. "I will speak with King Herod and attempt to calm him."

Lucius headed into the palace to witness the horrendous state of affairs.

Colorful carpets from Persia covered the marble floor of the throne room, a flashy, spacious chamber whose walls were overdecorated with gold and silver ornamentation. King Herod stormed about, yelling at his servants and guards.

"We MUST terminate the threat!" he yelled, his high-pitched voice screeching like a hawk. "I shall have NO ONE in this kingdom calling themselves a messiah!"

Despite his belligerence, King Herod was not a physically intimidating man. He was tall, but he was also skinny and gaunt, with a blanched pallor that made him seem undernourished. Like many Roman leaders, he maintained a clean-shaven face, which revealed a weak chin and low cheekbones. He had gangly arms with limp wrists that floundered as he walked about the room. And only a few lingering tufts of thin, white hair remained beneath his laurel wreath. If he had not inherited his high status from his father, he would have never ascended to the throne.

Lucius feigned ignorance as he entered the room.

"Oh, great King Herod," he said with a bow. "I saw evidence of a quarrel by the entrance to the palace. Pray tell, has something gone amiss?"

King Herod didn't even acknowledge the question. Instead, he rushed at Lucius, grabbed his throat, and pushed him against a wall. The king leaned in very close to the bureaucrat, as if he subconsciously desired a kiss.

"You must write to Rome IMMEDIATELY and demand they send troops! We must declare martial law!"

"Martial law?" Lucius gasped. "Why, what is the cause for this demand?"

"A BABY!" King Herod screamed. "The people are claiming A DAMNED BABY is the new messiah. He is a threat to my authority, and the authority of Rome!"

Lucius remained unfazed. He simply nodded and smiled.

"Yes, yes," Lucius agreed. "We must attend to this baby with great speed. Any potential messiah is a threat. Tell me, what do you know of this child?"

King Herod released Lucius and feverishly paced about the room.

"We have only heard rumors. The baby might have been born in Bethlehem in the last few days, but others say he was born as long as two years ago! All we know is that he's a baby."

"And you say Bethlehem?" Lucius continued. "That is an unlikely place for a messiah to be born...are you sure he is not elsewhere in Judea?"

King Herod shook his head. "Bethlehem is where the rumors were first reported, but we do not know for sure. Others say he was born in a holier city...perhaps even right here in Jerusalem!"

"Ah, yes! Jerusalem would make much more sense than Bethlehem," Lucius said, attempting deflection.

King Herod returned to his throne and looked out at the guards and servants before him, all of whom cowered mercifully.

"We must take swift action to eliminate the threat," King Herod called out to the room. "Guards, I command you to search EVERY house in Jerusalem, and then EVERY house in the rest of Judea. Locate EVERY baby boy under the age of two and kill them all! NO baby boy shall live! I command you to destroy this threat, all consequences be damned!"

The members of the court glanced at each other in terror. Murmurings filled the room, but King Herod would not tolerate dissent.

"DID YOU NOT HEAR ME?" he yelled, wrath radiating from his menacing glare. "I want you to kill all the male babies you can find in this kingdom, NOW!"

Bewildered, the guards and servants left the room, rushing off to determine the best way to handle the king's violent commands. Only Lucius and King Herod remained. Boldly, Lucius stepped forward to confront the king.

"My dear king, do you really believe such drastic action is necessary? This so-called messiah is still a baby. He likely cannot even speak! There is plenty of time to neutralize this threat before he becomes a true leader."

King Herod refused to look at Lucius. Instead, as he responded, he stared straight in front of him and spoke to the empty room in a petty and callous tone.

"I should like to remind anyone who might still be present that I am the King of Judea. My commands *must* be obeyed, even by diplomatic envoys from Rome."

Lucius relented—he would not waste his time. He bowed his head once again.

"Oh, great King Herod, forgive me! I could never doubt your brilliance. You are wise to react so decisively to this threat. And I shall tell my superiors in Rome of your gallantry. They will certainly be pleased!"

Lucius already knew his next step: no matter what happened to Baby Jesus, he would return to Rome with the urgent message that King Herod must be deposed. He would help develop a plan to assassinate the king in the most discrete manner, one that might suggest natural causes and prevent chaos in the kingdom. Some of his colleagues had orchestrated such plots before. After they heard his stories of King Herod, he knew they would be eager to act.

But first, he would have to warn the young couple staying in the stables at The Butterfly Sanctuary.

Lucius bowed again, turned his back on the king, and exited the room swiftly.

The sun was setting when Lucius arrived in Bethlehem. His horse galloped through the stone-laden streets back to the inn. The couple and their baby remained in the stables, but the courtyard of the inn lay empty, for the census had completed, and many travelers had already returned home.

Lucius ran inside and up the stairs to Abrahamus's room. He knocked on the door, and when it opened, he entered speedily.

"Hurry, we must act fast, Abrahamus! I need your help! The King of Judea is mad, and—"

He stopped mid-sentence, astounded by what he saw: Abrahamus stood beside the door, naked. His immense appendage dangled between his legs. Across the room, Prince Hamid lay in his bed, entirely undressed as well.

"Oh my! What is this? And you are still here, sir?" Lucius exclaimed, too bewildered to know who to address. "I figured you and your friends had already left!"

"Imran and Balbazaar departed this afternoon," Abrahamus said. "And the shepherds returned to their flocks. But thankfully, my beloved prince has chosen to stay a bit longer, to help teach me the many things that I have yet to learn..."

Lucius sat down on the floor, stunned.

"It is rare in this empire for male lovers to spend two consecutive nights together," he said.

Prince Hamid sat up in bed, the comforter barely concealing his midriff.

"It is also rare for two men to find a love like the one we have shared," he stated. "Abrahamus has been a gift from the Lord, and I am thankful to have his company."

Lucius took a moment to process the meaning of these words. In Rome, men rarely admitted to having anything more than superficial, carnal feelings for each other. To do so defied all conventions, not to mention the laws of the land. At times, he had felt deeper connections with other men and longed to have more meaningful engagements with them, but he always pushed those feelings away. Could two men truly love each other continuously?

Sadly, Lucius had no time to ponder such matters. He stood up and spoke with urgency to Abrahamus and Prince Hamid:

"I have some horrible news: the child who was born last night—the one you believe to be the son of God—he is in great danger. Word of the birth of a messiah reached King Herod, and he has turned mad with jealousy. He has commanded his troops to kill all baby boys throughout Judea, starting in Jerusalem. If we do not warn Mary and Joseph and help them escape, their child will meet an untimely death."

Prince Hamid shuddered. He had heard horrific tales of the tyranny of King Herod and knew everything Lucius said could very well be true.

"I will help them," Prince Hamid said. "I have traveled these lands far and wide, and I can guide them to safety. I can take them far away from here—to Egypt, perhaps—and make sure this newborn child lives."

Abrahamus walked to the bed and placed his hands on Prince Hamid's shoulders.

"If you must go," he said, "then take me with you. I have lived too long without you for you to leave so soon."

Prince Hamid looked up at the strong, muscular man who stood above him.

"Are you sure?" Prince Hamid asked. "The journey could prove dangerous. We might face guards from King Herod and have to fight to protect the child."

Abrahamus leaned forward and kissed Prince Hamid.

"Wherever you go, I must go, too. The time has come for me to leave this inn behind. If I stayed here without you, I would suffer. And I have anguished all alone for too long."

Prince Hamid smiled. "I was hoping you would say that. Wherever I go, I want you to come with me, too."

And the two kissed again, the long kiss of a certain and steadfast commitment. Lucius watched, his eyes watering with vicarious joy, for despite his many travels, he had never seen such pure, open, and wholesome love between two men.

"I see beauty in your love," Lucius said, "but you must leave tonight. A child's life is in danger. We do not know how soon King Herod might send his men to Bethlehem."

Abrahamus and Prince Hamid agreed. They quickly dressed and went down to the stables, where Mary, Joseph, and the Baby Jesus continued to rest. Lucius recounted the recent developments in Jerusalem, and they instantly agreed with the plan to escape. Abrahamus then went to Dinah and Laura and informed them of the situation, too.

"I am sorry to leave so suddenly," he said, "but I feel compelled to join this journey. Not only because I want to help this couple and their child, but also…because…"

His words drifted off, and he looked down at the ground. The old feelings of shame were rising in him again. Even though he knew Dinah and Lara had their own commitment, he still feared revealing his secret.

Dinah stepped forward and hugged Abrahamus.

"Oh, Abrahamus," she said. "We know. We saw you and that gentleman in the courtyard this morning, and we could see your happiness. You are leaving to go with him, aren't you?"

Abrahamus's eyes began to water. "Yes," he said.

Lara placed her hand on Abrahamus's arm.

"And do you love him?" she asked.

Abrahamus nodded eagerly. "Yes, I do! I love him very much!"

Lara burst into a smile. "Then this is great news and a great joy for us all!"

"We understand the urgency," Dinah said. "We always hoped that, someday, when you finally found your confidence, you might find somebody to love."

The two women hugged their protégé and gave him a tearful goodbye, knowing his departure might be permanent.

Abrahamus then hurried to the stables, where Prince Hamid had prepared both his horse and another one from the inn. Mary and Baby Jesus sat on the horse with Prince Hamid, ready to depart, while Joseph sat on the other, holding the harness for the mule that carried their belongings.

Lucius stood before them all, awed by the sight of these travelers and how fast they had assembled to save a baby.

"I must confess," he said to Abrahamus, as he gave him a platonic hug goodbye, "I have never seen two men have such a palpable connection and so much love. I am happy for you, and I can only hope and pray that someday, I, too, might find a love as strong and pure as yours."

Abrahamus smiled at Lucius. "Have faith in the Lord," he said. "The Lord brought Prince Hamid and me together. He gave us this joy. If you choose to believe in and commit to love, then I believe you shall find it, too."

Abrahamus joined Joseph, and the travelers disembarked, their horses and the mule trotting off into the night. They did not stop to rest, pressing on through the darkness, the dawn, the morning, and the afternoon, when they arrived at a seaside village on the Sinai Peninsula. There, Prince Hamid ensured Mary, Joseph, and the Baby Jesus could seek safe passage farther into Egypt. He and Abrahamus then rested for the remainder of the day. That night, they slept together on the beach, staring up at the stars.

The next morning, the men returned to Judea, circumventing both Jerusalem and Bethlehem to avoid attention. They continued on for three days and three nights, when they finally arrived in Osroene.

On the day of their arrival, Prince Hamid brought Abrahamus to his father, King Abgar Abgarid. And when he introduced him, he made no secret of the truth: Abrahamus was not only his new, most loyal advisor, but also his romantic partner.

Holding Abrahamus's hand, Prince Hamid stood before his father and spoke his truth:

"I need you to understand: this man is my soulmate. I love him most dearly. And I stand here before you and God, promising to commit to him, just as many other men commit to their wives. I will no longer involve myself romantically with any other man, and I shall never pursue women, for Abrahamus is the person I love more than anyone else in the world."

"I know we avoid such public admissions of this type of love," he continued. "Too many are inclined to treat such love as a forbidden secret. But I believe in the power of truth and honesty, and because an angel of the Lord reunited us, I know that God has blessed our union. If you object to our love, you can banish us from this kingdom, and we will take refuge in Rome or Iberia or some other faraway place. But no matter what, I intend to live with this man as though we are married. It is what the Lord wants. It is what Abrahamus wants. And it is what I want, too."

King Abgarid raised no objections. He clapped his hands and praised his son for delivering such a passionate speech, for he loved and respected his son, and he would never banish his own blood from his kingdom.

Abrahamus and Prince Hamid lived happily together in the Kingdom of Osroene. Although they maintained some discretion, their love was often displayed publicly. Occasionally, when they kissed or embraced before others, they agitated a prude, but even those naysayers soon came to realize that the power of their love was unstoppable and pure.

For forty years, the lovers maintained a merry union, until they passed peaceably of old age, eternally blessed and always loving one another.

Conclusion: A Theological Discussion

Having finished the story and extracted himself from Tybel's mouth, Daddy Santa rested next to his favorite elf. He gently stroked Tybel's sculpted body.

"So, you see," Daddy Santa said, "it was the gays who saved Baby Jesus. If it weren't for the love and devotion of Abrahamus and Prince Hamid, there might have never been another Christmas after the first Christmas."

Tybel kissed the nape of Daddy Santa's neck.

"It is a beautiful, sexy story," Tybel said, "And I now feel more strongly than ever that the world must hear it!"

Daddy Santa flinched.

"You absolutely must not share this story with anyone except other gay men you can trust! It must remain a secret. Why, if the true story of Baby Jesus were to ever leave the protection of the gays, it would cause chaos amongst the heterosexual population! People would be shocked! Offended! Humiliated!"

"What, exactly, is so offensive about this story?" Tybel asked. "The possibility that some men in ancient Judea had an orgy? Why, that was happening in Rome nearly every day! Nothing in your story is more humiliating than the person recently elected as the President of the United States of America!"

Daddy Santa scratched his chin. "Now, wait, do you mean President Biden or President Trump?"

Tybel sighed. "The fact that you have to ask speaks volumes. There are so many broken things in the world today—greed, disease, corruption, injustice—and gay sex has nothing to do with any of them. Gay love between consenting adults does not impact anyone besides the lovers themselves. Even when the sex is bad, nobody gets hurt!"

"But I think you know, Tybel," Daddy Santa said, "that putting homosexuality aside, there are passages in the Bible that say how adultery and sex without commitment are sinful. Doesn't this story put those sinners on a pedestal?"

"Perhaps some of the gay men who saved Baby Jesus had a few indiscretions," Tybel replied. "Perhaps we are sinners, too, even if Mrs. Claus permits you to experiment outside your marriage. But whether or not someone is a sinner is a matter between that person and their faith. And the sins of others do not justify the total erasure of gay sex from history! Sometimes, we must accept that things that make us uncomfortable exist and are beyond our control. And instead of dwelling so heavily on sin, perhaps we should focus our attention on the ways we can be joyful—on all the good and wonderful things the world has to offer."

Daddy Santa gave Tybel a forlorn look. "Do you really believe that our love might be sinful?"

Tybel kissed Daddy Santa on the cheek.

"Personally, I believe that if your love is caring, honest, and joyful, it is not a sin. From what I recall from Religion class at Elf School, the Bible is littered with examples of polyamory, and the text never explicitly forbids multiple commitments. So, in my humble opinion, having two committed partners is not inherently wrong. But this can only be true if you prove your commitment to me. You could start by opening up about our love, and also telling the world the story of the beautiful, gay love that existed in ancient Bethlehem…"

"But what about those few, pesky verses in the Bible that call homosexuality a sin? Don't those verses mean that gay love is always wrong, no matter how pure?"

"You must know that interpretations of those verses vary greatly," Tybel replied. "Some are viewed as mistranslations, and some are not even about consensual gay love in the first place. But those details aside, the Bible often warns of the dangers of loneliness. Isn't a loving commitment that lasted for decades worthy of celebration, not admonition?"

"But what if we are wrong about all of this?" Daddy Santa asked, quivering with fear. "What if our telling the world the truth about the first Christmas *does* lead to the collapse of Western Civilization, as so many fear?"

Tybel rolled his eyes.

"Honey, if Western Civilization is that flimsy, then maybe it isn't as important or mighty as people claim. And frankly, I doubt Western Civilization—whatever that means—will be going anywhere anytime soon, for better or worse."

Daddy Santa thought long and hard about Tybel's comments—longer and harder than his toy had been just a few minutes earlier! He looked longingly into Tybel's pleading eyes. He could see that Tybel wanted him so badly—wanted their love to be affirmed by the world, in spite of all the obstacles.

Finally, Daddy Santa smiled.

"Tybel, you have changed my mind," he said. "You are right. We must tell the world about both our love and the gay love that existed in Bethlehem during the first Christmas!"

Tybel squealed with delight. He grabbed Daddy Santa by the beard and smooched him on the lips.

"Oh, thank you, Daddy Santa!" Tybel shouted, bursting with joy. "Thank you, thank you, thank you! This is the best Christmas gift that I ever could have received."

"And receive you shall," Daddy Santa said with a wink. "It is my most sincere pleasure!"

"But how do we break the news to the world? And how will you tell Mrs. Claus? Are we sure she will be fine with us going public about our relationship?"

Daddy Santa rubbed Tybel on the back lovingly.

"Let me handle Mrs. Claus," he said. "Don't worry about her. I am confident she will understand. As for the rest of the world…I think I know the best way for us to spread our good news."

"What's your plan?"

"Well, recently, I have been looking into self-publishing e-books on the internet. It's a surprisingly easy process. Rather than trying to tell these stories verbally as men have done for generations, I think I will write them down and publish them under a pseudonym. Perhaps I could use a silly pen name—something suggestive!"

"That's brilliant, Daddy Santa! An e-book! Stories can move fast and go viral on the Internet, so we could hopefully share our story widely."

"Yes, we must spread our story widely—wider than I've ever spread your legs!"

Tybel and Daddy Santa snickered.

"And after people read this book," Daddy Santa continued, "they can help share this true story of Christmas and gay love, too! Readers should do all they can to tell others about our e-book—write positive reviews on the various book websites, post links to the e-book on social media, and tell any friends and family about this book! Doing so will help erase all the taboos around Christianity and gay love, too, for people should not live in fear of them."

"Yes, it is the readers who will help share the gay love of the first Christmas," Tybel added. "And I have faith in them. They can help spread the story of our love, and the story of the gayest love ever found in Bethlehem—a love that saved Christmas, too."

And Daddy Santa and Tybel embraced one another once again, filled with the joy that their story would soon be published on the internet, and that you, dear reader, would help spread the good news: that all love is love, and that the power of love—whether gay or straight—is the magic that makes our Christmas dreams come true.

The End

Acknowledgements

This book would not have been possible without the support of many friends and family. I give my full gratitude to my dear friends Marcy, Rebecca, and Pammy, who provided support, encouragement, and feedback at key moments during the creation of this book.

To my family: thank you for always accepting me for who I am. Your values have bolstered my faith. And thank you for embracing my decision to write LGBTQ+ Christian-themed erotic romance novels.

To my centenarian grandmother, who read the first edition of this book and described it as "ludicrously hot," thank you for always having an open heart and an open mind.

And to the readers who have found joy in the story of Abrahamus and Prince Hamid: thank you, too. I encourage you to spread the word and help others find pleasure in this novella!

A Brief Interview with Reverend Hard

Are you an actual Reverend? And is Richard B. Hard your real name, or is that just a pen name?

I do use a pseudonym for my books, but I am a minister ordained by the Universal Life Church.

What inspired *O, Gayest Love of Bethlehem*?

I wrote this book to offer readers a few laughs, some Christmas joy, and plenty of pleasure. However, I also wanted to tell a story of gayness in Biblical times. Although the labels we use to describe sexuality are a modern creation, LGBTQ+ people have always existed. Therefore, as Milton and Dante did in their times, I wanted to expand upon existing Christian narratives with my own angle: the inclusion of LGBTQ+ characters, along with some steamy moments!

Is this book fiction?

Yes—or, is it? Readers should note that the story remains fairly consistent with the Biblical account of the birth of Jesus. Until we have definitive proof that the innkeeper, the wise men, the shepherds, and King Herod were straight, we cannot rule out the possibility that this story might be true.

Does the discussion of so much sexuality, polyamory, and potentially sinful acts make this book blasphemous?

I'm sorry, have you read the Bible?

How is it possible for someone to be both LGBTQ+ and Christian? Doesn't the Bible condemn homosexuality?

There are many varying interpretations of the Bible. Many Christian churches and denominations around the world welcome gay congregants and fully embrace and accept members of the LGBTQ+ community. In reality, the Bible says very little about LGBTQ+ issues. However, the book extensively discusses values of faith, compassion, love, truth, justice, and authenticity. Letting people live their lives as their true selves aligns with those values.

Numerous scholars have written at length about the many ways we can interpret the Bible as affirming of the LGBTQ+ community. However, I prefer to refer folks to Matthew 19:12, a verse in which Jesus accepts and acknowledges "eunuchs…so born from their mother's womb." If Jesus were alive today, I believe he would embrace all genders and sexual orientations.

Did you write this book to try and convert LGBTQ+ people and other readers to Christianity?

No. I do not believe in evangelicalism. As a progressive Christian who believes in universalism, I think spiritual truths can be found in various faith traditions.

I also believe some people can live spiritually fulfilling and moral lives without adhering to any particular religion. People should pursue the spiritual path that resonates with them, and that is a journey that individuals should navigate freely and without coercion.

What is your favorite color?

Forest green, like the leaves in springtime.

What are some other resources to learn more about LGBTQ+ issues and Christianity?

Here are a few resources that I have found valuable:

- *Torn: Rescuing the Gospel from the Gays-vs.-Christians Debate* by Justin Lee
- *God and the Gay Christian: The Biblical Case in Support of Same-Sex Relationships* by Matthew Vines
- *1946: The Mistranslation that Shifted a Culture*, a documentary directed by Sharon Roggio

Please note that I am in no way affiliated with the creators of these resources, nor are they affiliated with me or this book. I do not necessarily endorse all their beliefs, and they do not necessarily agree with my views or support this book. I am only mentioning these resources as a way to help any LGBTQ+ individuals who are struggling spiritually.

What can we expect next from Reverend Hard?

Funny you should ask—I have a preview on the next page!

One final question…even after reading this book and your responses in this interview, I still feel ambivalent about everything. Is this book silly or sincere? What the heck is your deal anyway?

Let's not overthink things too much. At the end of the day, I am merely a humble reverend who enjoys indulging in a little bit of gay erotic romance. Sometimes, a story can contain qualities that are both silly and sincere. Some of the best stories are left open to interpretation. Whatever makes you feel the most joy, choose to interpret my writing in that way!

Coming Soon…

Intrigued? Visit www.RevRichHard.com and sign up for Reverend Hard's email list so you can be the first to learn more about future books!

About the Author

Reverend Richard Bartholomew Hard is a devout practitioner of his faith. He lives in Southern California, where he spends his time reading, writing, praying, and indulging in fantasies. He lives a private life, but he is happy to respond to inquiries through his website.

Learn more and sign up for email updates at his website:

www.RevRichHard.com

Make sure to follow Reverend Hard on social media:

- Instagram: @RevRichHard
- TikTok: @revrichhard
- Twitter: @RevRichHard
- BlueSky: @revrichhard.bsky.social
- Threads: @revrichhard
- Facebook Page: Reverend Richard B. Hard